THE LIGHT

W. J. Lundy

The Light

V6142016

Cover design by Eloise Knapp Design.

Chapter 1

Jacob sat beside her, trying to imagine the world being peaceful again; no more killing, no more monsters. A place where he could shower, watch TV, enjoy a good meal, and sleep in a warm bed. A dark night sky, the crisp winter air, the backyard's green grass coated with the light dusting of early snow. He forced his eyes closed, exhaled a long stream of white vapor, and felt her warmth against him, the blanket tight over their legs. Her body pressed against his on the bench, he wanted nothing more than to pull the blanket over their heads, just sit peacefully in his backyard, and pretend that none of this was happening.

His eyes drifted to the sky as he wrapped his arms around her shoulders. She pushed back, leaning her head against his neck, both of them ignoring what was clearly in front of them. He fought against the despair that was pushing into his chest, the eagerness to submit.

Not again; why can't it go back to the way it was?

Sitting in the backyard of his newly assigned military housing, for a brief moment the war felt far away. In this home with all the conveniences of their previous life, he wanted to ignore the metallic balloons flying high in the sky, but there was no mistaking what they were. This was The Darkness. It was back.

Jacob felt her tremble against him. He forced his head back, prying his eyes open and taking in the sight of the bright golden balls of light drifting across the sky. They slowed, the burning globes trailing vapor that quickly dissipated. No longer shooting stars, they now appeared solid, glowing bright, their bodies sharply in contrast against the night sky. It was hard to discern if they were small and floating low, or very large and soaring extremely high. As the UFOs lost altitude, they spread out, some slowly fading over the horizon as others settled directly overhead, eventually stopping right above the remote military base.

Jacob felt Laura press close against him under the blanket. Her arms shook; not from the cold, but the fear. Porch lights came on in the neighboring townhouses. Voices interrupted the silent night as people entered their backyards, searching the sky. He could hear the murmur of their speech, sensing the building panic. Months ago such an event would be cause for excitement, but not now. A phone rang from inside. Laura tensed and went to stand. Jacob put a hand on her leg, stopping her. "We have a phone?" he asked.

Laura grinned softly. "It only works inside the base, but all of us have one." She pulled away, removing the blanket from her legs. "I have to answer it; they only call in emergencies."

She stood and looked up at the sky before moving toward the house. Jacob was swiftly on his feet and following her through the sliding glass door, taking a last look at the alien globes before passing inside.

The old-style phone tolled until Laura lifted it from the cradle. Not speaking, she pressed the receiver to her ear. He watched as her flat expression changed to worry. She put a hand over the bottom of the handset and stared at Jacob. "He wants to speak to you," she said.

Jacob sighed and proceeded into the room, already dreading the message on the other side of the phone line. He took it from Laura and felt her hand on his back as she moved past him to the window, her eyes returning to the sky. Jacob turned away to face the wall, pressed the receiver to his ear, and swallowed.

"Jacob?"

"I'm here."

"This is Rogers. Do you see what's happening?"

Jacob nodded involuntarily. *Of course I see it, how could I not*? he thought to himself. "Yes. What is it?"

"They don't know yet, but these objects have taken out every satellite we had left in orbit. They've cast a virtual net over the entire planet, slowing and dropping in altitude, destroying all of our eyes in the sky—"

Laura stepped away from the window, turning to face Jacob. "They've stopped," she said. "They stopped moving."

"Europe ... Asia ... it's everywhere, all reporting the same phenomenon—"

"Come on, Rogers, we could use terms like that a year ago; this is The Darkness and you know it. Why did you call?"

"Listen to me. Get your family ready to move in a hurry, okay—"

"Wait, what are you saying … what do you know?"

"Nothing yet; nobody's saying anything, but have your family ready to go. We're bugging out. I'm headed to the hospital to find James. We'll stop at your place on the way back. Listen to what I said—have a bag packed and be ready to go."

"Come on, tell me what you think. What do you know?"

"If you were assaulting a base and were getting ready to bomb the hell out of it, what would you do with your troops just outside the fences?"

"Well … I'd move them away, get them in cover."

"Jacob, be quiet and listen now. The Deltas ... they started backing away from the walls less than an hour before these things showed up. It's like a button was pressed and they all turned around-—"

"Wait, where are they going?"

"Away, Jacob. We can't track them because they took out our satellites. They are turning and moving away. At first, command thought they were just retreating to the wood lines, but then we got word from other bases in NATO and holdouts out west. All of the Deltas are pulling back from major installations. Anywhere globes have been spotted, the

Deltas have withdrawn. There isn't a lot of time ... have your family ready. I'll see you soon."

The line went dead with a heavy click. Jacob held the phone in his sweaty palm, turning it in his hand, wondering about the warning. Debating in his mind, *Why else would the Deltas move away? They're going to bomb us.*

He carefully returned the receiver to its cradle and paced across the room. Stopping next to Laura, keeping her back to his chest, he put his arms around her.

"Are you leaving again?" she asked.

"I'm not sure. I need you to pack a bag for us."

"Us?"

She reached down and grabbed his hands, pulling them tight around her waist. "It's already done. The men from your unit showed me how to pack a bag in case we had to leave in a hurry. It has clothes, some food and water, even extra ammunition for the rifle … I packed everything they put on the list. It's in the hall closet."

Jacob smiled, impressed with her. "We aren't the same people anymore, are we?"

She shook her head and sighed. “I don’t want to be caught like that again, like what happened in Chicago.”

“I don’t either.”

She paused, looking away at the night sky. Her voice softened. “What did you see out there? Is it bad?”

“It’s the worst.”

“Then where will we go?”

Jacob held his breath, not knowing. He pressed his eyes closed and exhaled. “I don’t know. But the people I left with, they’re the good ones. I’ll follow them.”

“You trust them?”

Jacob paused, considering his answer. He had as much to lose as they did. They had no reason or motive to help him; in fact, they would be better off without him and his family to slow them down. The men had nothing but each other. Jacob considered her question. “Yes, they’re part of our family now. They’ll be here soon, you’ll see.”

***

The remains of Alpha squad, the Assassins, arrived three hours later with an impatient knock. When Jacob opened the door, it was still night. The golden globes put off an eerie glow that lit the street in an orange hue. He stepped onto the front stoop and looked up at the sky.

"Like jack-o-lanterns, aren't they?" Rogers said.

He turned his gaze, finding them all there. Jesse, loopy from pain killers and his neck still wrapped. James, with his new scout dog, Duke, close beside them, were standing near the driveway. The bearded man knelt down and rubbed the dog's ears. A late model Chevy Blazer painted in a woodland camouflage pattern—the replacement for the green military Jeep—sat parked on the street, a matching pickup truck just behind it.

"Well? You going to invite us in?" James shouted.

"Yes, of course. Come on, guys, get in here."

Jacob backed away, pulling the door open while they pushed in past him just as Laura drifted down the stairs from the second floor. Spotting them, she greeted them and introduced herself at the threshold. "Please … everyone come in, I'll put on some coffee."

James's ears perked up. "Coffee? How about a beer?"

Biting her lower lip, Laura stared at the bearded man. Jacob stepped between them. "Ignore this guy. Coffee would be great, hun," he said, ushering the men into the next room.

Laura nodded with a smile and turned away from them as the team worked their way into the small sitting room. With his back resting against the wall, Jacob watched them all find places around the sparsely furnished home. They were in better shape than the last time he saw them, cleaned up and in fresh uniforms. Jacob retrieved a chair from the dining room and brought it near the others.

Katy appeared at the top of the steps and looked down wearily, rubbing her eyes. Jacob was on his feet and fetched her, bringing her back to the sitting room with him. Laura returned and was handing out small cups of coffee. "Wish we could offer more, but the rations …" she said, setting the pot and tray of cups on a small table before quickly moving to her husband's side.

Rogers grinned and dipped his head as he raised a cup. "Jacob, we need to talk about our next move."

Katy squirmed trying to escape Jacob's arms, having taken notice of Duke across the room, curled into a ball at James's feet. She pulled away and fell in beside the dog. James hoisted Katy onto his knee as the little girl tugged and yanked at Duke's ears, Duke leaning into it and enjoying the child's attention.

Jacob turned back to Rogers. "What's the plan?"

"We don't have an officer; our unit is on standby until they find a replacement for—" Rogers paused and swallowed hard. "We are on hold until we get a new CO. They want to keep us on the base, but I fought and finally got permission for us to refit at the outpost. I don't think it's safe here, or at least it won't be shortly."

Laura looked at Rogers. "The outpost?"

Rogers nodded. "A set of cabins close to here. It's a safe place."

Jacob stared at James, who appeared discouraged as he sat holding Katy and the dog leaning into them. "Where are Eve and the old man?" Jacob asked.

Rogers dipped his head and grinned. "They're safe, caught a resupply bird back to the bunker an hour ago."

"Well, maybe we should go there," Jacob said.

"No; no way command would okay it. The outpost will work for now. Just an hour from here, it's secluded. We have everything we need: a full pantry, fresh water source, shelter, and good communications. In reality, we have better access there than we do here."

James shook his head. "Give me half a day; I'll go secure us a bird and we can—"

Rogers took a deep breath. "I know, James, and we'll get there. Listen, I read Captain Cole's last report from the bunker. The dioxin is still holding the Deltas back. No reported pumpkin sightings since we left the area. Cole has a fire team holding there. Gloria and the kids are safe. It sounds ideal, but I'm not ready to just go rogue … not yet. And you know if we show up uninvited, Cole will send us back."

James sat Katy down next to Duke and tossed up his hands. "Regardless, we need to get back. We should leave tonight while we're all still in the clear," he said. "Come on, man, you know things are about to go sideways. You willing to risk it all?"

Rogers clenched his jaw. "I'm working on it. I plan to get us all there in due time, but for now, making it to the outpost is the best play."

Jacob reached to the window and drew back the curtain. Changing the subject, he asked, "So what are they?"

Rogers shook his head. "Don't know. Space command tracked them coming in from behind the moon. They seemed to hit from all angles at once then slowed down as they entered the atmosphere.

"Now they're floating and spreading over population centers. We have three over us right now. The Russians hit one with an S-300, knocked the hell out of it and forced it down. They sent out a recon team to investigate, but we haven't heard back. Our people in Texas wagered a shot at one with a Patriot battery; let them have it good, multiple missile hits. Last report is the thing went down somewhere off the shore of Corpus Christi."

"So they didn't fight back?" Jacob asked.

"No, but …"

"But what?" Jacob asked.

"In both cases, after they shot one down, it was replaced by two more in a higher orbit, and the second group has managed to evade the missiles," Rogers said.

"Probes." James turned to look at Jacob. "They learn, they adapt, and now they know our anti–air capabilities."

"So that's it, that's all we have?" Laura asked.

James nodded, smiling at Katy playing with the dog. “That’s all we know.”

Rogers finished the rest of his coffee and stood, placing the empty cup on the table. “We should get going. Once we get to the outpost, I can talk to the pilots and arrange transportation to Stone’s bunker from there. We have a helicopter pad on a hill nearby with a fully fueled helicopter if things go the way we think they will. I’m sure it won’t take much convincing for the pilots to bug out with us.”

Chapter 2

The vehicles were fully loaded with supplies. Under the cover of darkness, they rolled through the gates of the Assassins unit's compound on the far side of the base. Jacob was pressed in the cab of the pickup truck with Laura sitting in the center of the bench seat and Katy on his lap.

Rogers looked over at him from the driver's seat. "We have two trailers already loaded with gear; we're just going to get them hitched and we'll be on our way," he said.

The big man stepped out of the truck and ran into the dark night. The engine remained running, the headlights on and illuminating the sides of a steel-walled building. Jacob rolled down his window, allowing the cool air mixed with diesel exhaust to enter the vehicle. Katy was curled into his lap, her head against his chest. Looking out, Jacob could see the globes; three of them were positioned over the base, still glowing and passing off their dull, orange light. He looked left and right, following the horizon.

The globes positioned themselves directly overhead. Jacob felt the fear in his chest, and he suddenly wanted to be far away from them. *Rogers was correct about leaving,* he thought.

"Hey, give us a hand," he heard James shout from outside.

Jacob grimaced and slid Katy from his lap, handing her off to Laura before he opened the door and left the truck. Rogers and James were wrestling with a large green trailer. It was fastened to a type of dolly, which the men were using to push it across the lot and fasten it to the backs of the vehicles. With Rogers up front guiding it, Jacob put his hands on the back beside James and helped push it forward.

"What's in here?" Jacob asked, grunting.

James laughed. "Everything. When he got back earlier," James said dipping his head toward Rogers, "right after the pumpkins showed up, Rogers emptied the team rooms into these two trailers. You know how he is … the guy is like a boy scout, always prepared."

With a flicker of light, everything changed. The dull glow overhead intensified. When Jacob looked back to the sky, the globes directly above them were turning a deep red. Looking directly at it, he could feel the radiant heat. Then slowly the orb climbed in altitude as it began to rotate.

Rogers saw it too and, slapping down the top hook and securing the hitch with a pin, said, "We need to move. Back to the trucks."

Jacob proceeded to the front of the vehicle and jumped into the cab, pulling the door shut behind him. Looking up, he watched as the bottom of the nearest globe turned to black then fired. Not the way Jacob imagined it would, with lasers or cannons suddenly extending from the top, or maybe missiles launching from holes twisting toward earth in tiny spirals. None of that. The globes changed color then slowly rotated clockwise, the bottoms opened up revealing a blue light, and then they dropped a tiny seed. He couldn't take his eyes off the rotating orb.

"Something is falling out of it," he uttered.

Jacob stretched back, holding tight and pressing his head out of the rear window. The truck rocketed forward at high speed close behind James as he aquired the lead in the Blazer, the vehicles whipping through the gates of the unit compound, racing onto a gravel road, tossing loose stone in their wakes.

He watched the seed spiral down, dropping out of view just above the surface of the ground. Then the earth trembled.

"Look away from it!" Rogers yelled.

Jacob ducked inside and grasped a hand across his face an instant before a bright flash erupted in the distance. He pulled Laura and Katy down to his legs, shielding them from the light, both of the girls now screaming. Looking over, he saw Rogers's jaw was clenched, his left hand over his face as he stayed on the throttle and focused on keeping the truck straight on the road.

After the flash, a blinding cloud of debris crashed and overtook the vehicles. They were now driving through a thick fog of dust, the headlights barely illuminating the way ahead. Blinded, James was forced to slow down while Rogers moved the truck forward, staying in view of the lead vehicle's taillights.

"What was that … a nuke?" Laura asked, her voice trembling. Katy was still in her arms, sobbing.

Rogers shook his head, both hands clutching the wheel tight. "I don't think so; we'd be dead if it were. Maybe kinetic … electrical? A rail gun firing straight down, fuck … something unknown?"

Jacob looked back behind them, trying to focus on anything in the cloud of thick dust through the rear window. "I think they hit the airfield."

Rogers nodded his head. "Most likely."

"You think anyone got out?" Laura asked.

Rogers clenched his jaw and narrowly shook his head, not taking his eyes off the Blazer in front of him. "There were three of them in our area; the globes probably placed themselves so they would have overlapping blast radiuses. We were five … maybe ten miles away when they hit. You felt the blast and shockwaves yourself. What can you imagine happened closer?"

Suddenly the truck ahead stopped, the taillights growing bright. Rogers slapped the truck into park. The girls got very quiet as a spotlight hit the windshield, cutting through the haze. Neither Rogers nor Jacob spoke as a group of men with flashlights patrolled up both sides of the road, rifles aimed at the cab. Rogers lowered his window and leaned out. "Slow your roll, heroes, and get those damn rifles out of my face; I got a kid in here."

The lead soldier put up a hand, waving the others off, then approached the driver's window. He saw the rank on Rogers's collar. "Sorry, Sergeant, we're all on edge. What the hell happened?"

Rogers's own eyes showed alarm. He looked across at Jacob then back at the soldier. "I don't know. Do you have contact with the other stations, other gates?"

"No, Sergeant, the radio fuzzed out just before those things turned red … then the blast … You all are the first vehicle we've seen. Are there any more behind you?"

"I don't think so. We were already on the road when they attacked. Listen, secure this gate, do what you can to lock it up then get your people out of here. Whatever they did back there, I'd say this position is no longer worth defending."

The soldier's eyes went wide as he looked past the truck and down the road toward the main base. "But, Sergeant, I can't just abandon the post; I—I've got orders," the soldier said.

"Look, I can't make you leave, but I would highly recommend you do what I say. Find a place to hole up, someplace hidden back in the trees to watch the base from cover if you want. Try to stay on the radio, but just get the hell out of the open, okay?"

Rogers pointed ahead as the Blazer began to ease forward, showing James's eagerness to leave. "We've got to go. There is a mission staging area not far from here, do you know it?"

"Yes, Sergeant. O.P. Thunder."

"That's right. If you can, try to get there," Rogers said.

Rogers placed the truck into gear and rolled ahead after the lead vehicle. As the truck trekked forward, Jacob spied through the windows, making eye contact with the frightened and dirt-covered faces of the guard force. He wondered if they saw the same fear in his own eyes. The truck trudged over a rise in the road and snaked around concrete barriers before moving out onto the open roadway.

***

The fallout settled, and the sun burned off the heavy condensation, clearing the air. Jacob searched the sky but couldn't find any of the globes. They rounded a corner and traveled north at a fork in the road. Laura was asleep next to him with Katy still in her lap. Off to the right, Jacob saw plumes of black smoke in the sky. He pointed at it silently, Rogers catching the signal.

"That over there is probably the closest thing to a big city around here," Rogers said. "It's a small village, maybe a hundred homes, some small shops."

"You think they bombed it too?" Jacob asked.

"Maybe … or the residents are panicking, nearby refugees looting what's left. Most of these areas up north were unscathed by the Deltas. The local military did a great job cordoning off the bigger towns and villages.

"But what we saw last night. That's a game changer. I'm sure there are a lot of scared people this morning."

Laura turned her head and opened her eyes. With a groggy expression, she glanced at Jacob then down at Katy. "How much longer?"

Following the Blazer, they turned onto another dirt road entering a sparse forest. "We'll be there soon," Jacob said.

Katy wiggled awake and scrambled, trying to sit up. She reached out for Jacob, who raised her back onto his lap. "Are we going home, Daddy?"

Jacob grinned. "Not yet, but we're going to a cabin in the woods, just like when we went camping."

She smiled and pressed her head against the window, watching as the trees passed by. Laura dug through a small bag at her feet and retrieved a bottle of water. Opening it, she took a sip before placing it in Katy's hands then watched the road ahead of them as the thick tree cover blocked out the light. The road narrowed, becoming barely wide enough for two vehicles to pass.

The sides of the road banked up steeply. They occasionally passed a house or small hunting cabins with boarded up windows. Rogers explained that there were very few homes in the area; most of the places there were seasonal and empty now. If people were living in them, they did a fine job of making the places look vacant. Most people from the towns and large cites didn't have interest in the harsh backwoods. Even refugees traveling long distances from the camps tended to avoid the rough terrain. The forest isn't inviting like a farm or small village, where people imagined they could easily take animals or food from the fields. The woods required skill and could be very unforgiving to the untrained.

Rogers pointed to an abandoned vehicle on the roadside with the doors and trunk open. "City folks like to imagine they can survive out here deep in the woods, like they'll live off berries and mushrooms. A rabbit in every pot, shit like that. In the months after the fall, I buried a lot of their kind."

They rode silent for a few minutes before Laura spoke again. "Are the others here?" she asked. "Those … things?"

"The others? You mean the Deltas?" Rogers answered.

"Yeah. They were at the fences yesterday. Where did they go?"

Rogers scowled. "Those were on the south walls; the north side of the base was clear. We're traveling through what we called the western corridor. It's a heavily patrolled, small tract of land barely five miles wide and flanked by some very tough terrain. This is the only route we had from the base back to the ports and to reach the States."

"The only route?"

"Except by air, of course."

"So this place, the cabin, it's in the corridor? It's protected?"

The truck slowed as the Blazer in front came to a complete stop, and then edged forward onto a narrow driveway almost entirely concealed by heavy vegetation. The gravel road became an unmaintained rutted trail leaving the forest road behind. At first the driveway appeared invisible. The soldiers who stayed here covered it with large swaths of pine needles and dry leaves then left a zigzagging stretch of brush piles to conceal the entrance. The truck bounced and the shocks squeaked in protest. Katy let out a giggle as she was rocked up and down on Jacob's lap.

"Yes," Rogers said, continuing, "this is still in the defense corridor, but I don't know the state of it after the attacks. We're secluded enough; in fact, we are about as far away from things as we can get. That should buy us some time."

She turned and looked to Jacob with concern, then back to Rogers. "How much time?"

Rogers maneuvered the truck into the yard of the cabin and killed the engine. He let out a loud frustrated sigh. “I don’t know; that depends on what else those pumpkins brought us.”

Chapter 3

"Well, it's not much to look at," Laura said, holding a bag with Katy next to her. Jacob stood beside them, his rifle slung over his shoulder and Laura's rifle in his free hand. James moved up with Duke, the dog running to Katy and pressing against her, begging for more attention. At the top of the grassy hill they were standing on stood the one-room cabin named O.P. Thunder. A tall barn was just behind it.

James pointed at a small trail that ran to the barn then curved off behind it. "What you see is only the main house. Used to be some sort of vacation place up here. This was a reception place, lobby, or something. There are several smaller cabins off that trail. Each is connected to the main house by a sound-powered telephone. Take it far enough, you'll find a lake and hunting lodge.

"The lodge is surrounded by open prairie; that's where they keep a couple helicopters and a drunk-ass—" James paused, looked down at Katy, and cleared his throat. "Excuse me, our *pilot* likes to stay up there. Keep going all the way to the top of the hill, there's a radio tower and on the far side is a small town. Same one we saw on our way here."

Laura followed his hand then looked back at the larger cabin. "Where are we staying?"

Jacob's head came up and he raised a hand toward the main building. "Best if we all stay up here for now."

As a group they proceeded up to the main house, Jacob observing the grounds while the rest gathered. The last time he was here it was dark and gloomy from a downpour. The constant falling of the rain and the pending mission had given him tunnel vision; he hardly recognized the place in the bright sunlight. They stepped onto the covered front porch and entered the cabin.

The space smelled of hickory and wood smoke even though the fireplace was cold. Cast iron pots and kettles were neatly stacked on a shelf near the mantle. While the others selected the far wall, Rogers pointed to a corner of the cabin where the only bed was located and told Laura she could occupy that space with Katy. Looking at Jacob, she started to protest. Rogers smiled and said they wouldn't be getting much sleep anyhow, so it wasn't worth the discussion. After they all agreed, he showed them where they could keep their weapons and how to access the pantry and fresh water stores.

Jesse stumbled through the open room and sat heavily in a wooden rocking chair, still out of it, while Rogers led Jacob and James outside. They went to work unloading the gear from the trucks and storing it in the barn. The place was larger than Jacob remembered. Having only been inside the front door of the hay barn on his previous visit, he could now see that behind a large set of wooden doors it went back a depth of at least sixty feet and had high shelving on both sides. The shelves were stocked with cases of MREs and boxes with brand names he recognized from grocery stores. The back wall was completely filled with cases of water.

"The people on base were being rationed. Why is there so much here?" Jacob asked, carrying the last box of goods from the truck. He moved to a shelf and dropped the box on the straw-covered floor.

"This is just the Quartermaster's stash," Rogers said. "It's for units going down range. You didn't complain when we loaded your pack full of it last time."

"Where did it all come from?"

"We brought most of it with us when we withdrew from the States. The rest we stocked up on during supply runs. There's more too; we have a weapons and ordnance cache in a cave at the top of the hill by a radio tower."

Jacob passed the long rows of shelves then turned, looking at the full rucksacks lined up against a wall—obviously loaded for missions down range. "Why aren't there more people here?" he asked.

Rogers stopped and stared at the same row of packs. "Been asking myself the same question. They sent two platoons west after the dioxin. Maybe the rest were sent to defend the camp. Or the town over the ridge. Usually aren't more than a few teams here at a time, but I was still expecting to see a friendly face or two."

James crossed through the double doors and moved past them to a row of canned goods. He stopped and leaned against the shelving. "I think we need to patrol up the trail, make sure the birds are still there. Then … we should leave."

"I know," Rogers said. He exhaled and edged to a stack of empty pallets sitting on their edge. "We'll go, but we need to be suited up; I have a feeling those globes brought more than just bombs."

***

James led them out after lunch, patrolling up the hill. Jacob stepped in front of Rogers, watching James further ahead of him with Duke leading the way with his nose. He felt bad about leaving Katy and Laura alone with Jesse, but she understood. They were blind out here all alone, and she wanted to know the state of things just as bad as the rest of them did. Seeing the rifle slung over Laura's shoulder as she hugged him goodbye, Jacob was amazed at how their lives had changed—from hiding in a bedroom, to him going on patrols while she protected the camp.

The patrol's first objective was to check out the helicopter pad; then Rogers wanted to visit the radio tower overlook at the top of the ridge. He wanted to gather intel on the neighboring village; he needed to find out if it was really bombed and if not, why it was burning. The men still hadn't seen a globe since they left the base, and he was growing concerned the things may have landed. If they landed, he wanted to know what they brought with them. They were all thinking it was an invasion, yet none of them would say the words out loud.

Jacob patrolled forward, watching every step as he navigated the well-worn trail that was married to a ridge line. He could see the place was heavily used by tourists at some point; the sides of the trail were marked by posts indicating popular hiking paths that jutted off the main trail. At one open spot there were several wooden benches with names carved into it. Farther up, was a picnic area with tables and permanent barbecue pits. Jacob looked to the front and watched Duke trotting along with a relaxed posture, only occasionally stopping to stand point at a squirrel or sniff a raccoon track.

The team passed several identical small cabins, each of them rustic with a small covered porch and a single window in the front. The patrol checked the first two, stopping to peek inside and seeing the empty beds and cold wood stove. They were not only empty, but also bore no signs of people, or any clue they'd been used recently.

Just below the ridge line, the trail broke off to the south. A post in the ground indicated it would lead to an athletic field. James made the turn following the path and guided them onto a trail that doubled in width as it rounded a bend. Jacob could see bright sunlight breaking through the trees, indicating that the clearing was ahead. The point man put up a flat hand, then stepped off into the tall vegetation on the side of the trail. Jacob followed the guide's lead and knelt to the side as Rogers brushed past him to creep close to James.

Jacob adjusted his position so he could watch the back trail while the others planned. A breeze gently moved the trees and, lifting his face, Jacob smelled tobacco smoke. He turned his head as Rogers crept up beside him. Rogers held fingers to his lips, mimicking a cigarette, and pointed in the direction of the clearing. James looked back and waved them forward as he stepped up and led the way.

They moved into the clearing together, more relaxed knowing that the Deltas didn't smoke, but still on alert for strangers. The field was a bit larger than a double football field. A Blackhawk helicopter was at one end, its blades staked down and a cover tossed over much of the body of the aircraft. On the far side of the bird was a small block building and a covered picnic area. The building had a stone chimney climbing to the top and small patio in front of a covered open porch. To the right of the porch sat a man leaning back in a wooden chair. He had a vintage western cowboy hat resting low over his eyes, and his feet were up on a loose stack of split firewood.

As Jacob moved closer, he could see a cigarette in his right hand with a long smoldering ash.

"So what's his story?" Jacob whispered as they crept closer.

James turned his head, scanning before looking back ahead. "You mean Buck? He's a good cat. A Nam'er … retired in the early '90s. Guess he was on a beach down in Florida and somehow found his way up here driving a crash hawk after things went to shit. Don't get me wrong, Buck is a good catch. He knows his stuff, but he's a bit of a lush when it comes to the sauce."

The man in the cowboy hat shifted in his seat and let out a hacking cough, somehow startling Duke and causing the normally quiet dog to release a loud string of barks. The man kicked back with his boots and fell over in the chair. Rolling and scrambling to his feet, he fought against the straps of a holstered sidearm.

Jumping ahead with his hands up, Rogers announced, "Calm down, Buck, it's just us."

The silver-haired man relaxed, falling exhausted against the building, taking deep breaths while holding a hand over his heart and wiping sweat off his forehead with the other. "Dang, guys, I nearly killed all of ya. Ya can't go sneaking up on me like that."

"Wasn't much sneaking up. What the hell are you doing sleeping out here in the open, you old fool?" Rogers said.

The old man fanned his face with the hat. "Shoot, ain't nothing going on up here."

"You don't know about the attack, do you?" Rogers asked.

"What, on the fences? That's old news—"

"No, you old fool, the bomb drop. They bombed the base, blew it to hell."

Buck's arms went slack as his eyes focused on Rogers. "You mean," —he stopped and shook his head— "No … I heard an explosion last night; hell, it shook the cabin. But … no, that was just the zoomies on a run … it couldn't have come from that far away. Would have to be a nuke to feel a bomb's blast from that far away."

"Buck, something hit us. The globes—or whatever they are—they dropped something on the base. Something big." Rogers paused to look back at Jacob. "We barely escaped the blasts ourselves."

"No, that can't be," Buck said, moving back to the chair and dropping into the seat. He reached forward, searched between the bits of stacked wood, and retrieved a corked bottle. He removed the cap and took a long sip. "How bad was it?"

"We didn't go back to see," Rogers said. Changing the subject, he pointed at the helicopter. "Is it ready to go?"

Buck rolled his shoulders and focused his eyes on the single Blackhawk. "It's topped off if you need to go for a spin, but … the other birds haven't returned. I don't have a left seater, and no gunships. They recalled the chinook back to the base for maintenance yesterday … guess you explained why they haven't—"

Cutting him off, James stepped away from the porch and looked up the trail in the direction of the hilltop. "We need to keep moving if we want to get back before sundown."

Rogers nodded in agreement and turned back to Buck. "Get sobered up; we're patrolling up to the ridge. I need to check out the arms cache. Oh, and we saw fire in the village on the way in. You know anything about it?"

Buck shook his head no, removing his hat and dragging an arm over his forehead.

"Well, I want to know why it's burning."

"Well, hell, I'm sober now; maybe I'll tag along and have a look myself."

"Buck, I don't have time to argue with you. Get the bird ready to go, okay?"

Buck pulled his head back and nodded. "Can do."

Chapter 4

The trip to the top of the hill went without incident. They found the tower and cave entrance unguarded and unoccupied. Partially concealed by tall grass, the cave doors were sealed tight by steel bars going deep into the rock, broad hinges welded to the plate steel, and a cipher lock dead center. The cave wasn't well hidden; most of the structure protruded from the rock at the base of the hill, and fresh earth had been piled at the sides where it met with roughly poured concrete. Jacob walked past the doors and saw a large stack of discarded steel shelving, as well as other equipment cabinets.

"What is this place?" Jacob said.

Rogers stepped to the cipher lock and opened a plastic cover, revealing the face of the keys. "Used to be a maintenance locker for the radio and the phone companies use. They kept their computers and cell stuff in here. Some of it still is here. When the Army took ownership, they gutted most of the old, unusable stuff and reclaimed the floor space. There's a generator in the back, and most of the batteries are still good."

Jacob looked at the entrance; he could see the welds were new. He pounded on the door, feeling the heavy plates thump without an echo. "Why so much security up here, out of the way?"

James skirted past them with Duke at his side, stopping near a large boulder and dropping to his rear. "The bean counters at the base insisted on it; guess they were worried if the militias knew about this cache, they might try and grab some. We have people defecting from the units every day, so secrets are hard to keep," James said. He turned and looked at Rogers. "How we gonna get inside?"

Jacob stopped and glanced back at the lock. "You don't know the combination?" he asked incredulously.

Rogers sighed and dropped the plastic cover, letting it fall over the key pad. "Only officers had it. Marks had it, but ..." Rogers paused and shoved a hand into his pocket before looking back at the worried face of Jacob, "now I have it."

They grew quiet, remembering their fallen commander. A gunshot echoed from over the hill. Rogers's head lifted as he looked toward the summit. He stepped around the cave's bunker-like door and climbed up the steep face to the top of the hill.

Pausing at the top, he crouched low so that he wouldn't skyline himself against the sun. He turned and looked out along the far side. He crept ahead, focusing on something far in the distance, and then moved away. Jacob scrambled up behind him.

A cool breeze hit him in the face. He looked down into a long, green valley covered in thin trees. At the end of the valley, Jacob could barely make out the shapes of homes and other structures. Focusing on the center and far side of the village, he spotted a thin stream of black smoke.

"That the same village we passed on our way here?" Jacob asked, although knowing the answer.

Before Rogers could reply, they heard more sounds of gunfire—not just random shots, but open combat, automatic weapons fire joined by the thumps of distant explosions. Duke edged past them and stretched forward, his tail tucked and ears going ridged. He let out a subtle whine as James lifted his rifle and used the scope to look into the distance.

Joining the sounds of combat, an unfamiliar metallic clang echoed—like the smashing of metal drums—followed by a high-pitched *voomp, voomp, voomp*. Finally, a bright flash of light and a deafening explosion caused the ground to shudder. There was no shockwave, but the men could feel the heat of the light on their faces. The gunfire slowly diminished, and more smoke filled the distant skyline.

The village was in flames now, the black smoke being defused by a thicker cloud of gray that hung heavy on the ground, obscuring their view of the village.

Backing away, James shook his head side to side. He lowered his rifle. "That didn't sound like … like any weapon … any*thing* I know."

"Maybe a plane crash?" Jacob suggested.

"No," Rogers said. "Don't be stupid, you know what that was. They're under attack."

Waving for the others to follow, he moved back down the hill away from the smoke before stopping at the bunker door.

"They had a light garrison in that village, just enough to keep the Deltas away." Rogers lifted the plastic cover and keyed in the door's code. He moved his hand to the latch and pushed down, releasing the lock. The door swung out with a screech of metal on metal.

Jacob descended the hill and looked into the cavern. Shaped like the back of a semi-truck trailer, the space was no more than twelve feet wide but led into the rock farther than Jacob could see.

"Whatever just happened down there, that wasn't Deltas," James said.

Green weapons racks lined the walls and were filled with all sorts of small arms. Deeper in the corridor, beyond the racks, sat stacked cardboard boxes, lockers, and wooden crates painted in olive drab. Rogers hit a switch on the wall and paused as lights slowly flickered to life down the length of the bunker's ceiling. The farthest light revealed a small workstation on the back wall. Rogers didn't wait for the others and stamped directly to it. He tugged at a metal lock box and removed a ring filled with keys.

Rogers's normally calm demeanor was gone, and he now moved with a rigid purpose. He spun around and put the key to a lock on the nearest crate. He flipped open the lid and reached inside, removing a three-foot-long green cylinder. Rogers passed the first to Jacob then took a second in his hand before walking to the weapons racks. "What do you think, James? The M82?"

James moved in behind them and shrugged. "Yeah, that ought to do it."

"Wait," Jacob said. "What the hell is going on?"

Rogers ignored the question and opened a long, metal box, removing a large canvas bag. He turned and pointed at James. "Make sure it's good to go, no time to waste." The big man then turned back to Jacob and snatched the tube from his hands. He pulled at the side and adjusted the shoulder strap before handing it back. "This is an anti-tank rocket, AT4. Make sure you hold on to it."

Jacob put his hands up, refusing the rocket. "What's going on? Talk to me."

"We're going down to the village; we need to take a look."

Jacob shook his head. "With all of this," he said, pointing to the rocket. "Looks like more than taking a look."

"I'm not going to lie to you, Jacob. If we get the opportunity, I'll kill whatever made that sound."

"Shouldn't we go back and warn the others first? Why not just leave?"

"I'll call on the field phone and let them know we won't be home for dinner. As of now though, what would we warn them about? We don't know what's going on." He paused and shook his head, looking down at the ground before turning back. "I know running seems like the smart bet, but … Hell, just strap this to your pack; we're not leaving without answers," Rogers said, pushing the rocket into Jacob's chest. He then moved to the rear of the bunker, where he grabbed a green telephone handset from a cradle.

Jacob held the rocket loosely in front of him, watching as James lifted the heavy canvas bag to his back and adjusted shoulder straps, Duke waiting patiently at his heels. “Let’s go,” he said, winking at Jacob as he moved away and exited the space.

Chapter 5

Dropping down the sloping walls of the valley, the acrid odor of the smoke grew stronger. The sun fell into the clouds and the temperatures dropped. Rogers moved them cautiously, avoiding open spaces, leading them through thick grass, and copses of tall trees. The terrain became marshy and sponge-like. Even in the cold air, Jacob felt himself sweating, the pools of moisture forming at the back of his neck and running down his back beneath the small pack he was covered by.

The ground was wet here; he felt it squish under his boots with every step. Jacob took a short leap over standing water and felt his boot sink into the mud. He pulled it out, fighting the suction, and whispered, "Isn't there a better route?"

James looked back at him and grinned. "This is good; it'll make it hard for vehicles to maneuver against us."

"What vehicles?"

Rogers shot up a flat hand and crouched low in the grass. He looked back at the other two with wide eyes and put a finger to his ear. Duke's ears were pointed, the dog's lip quivering, letting the others know that he'd heard it too.

A low vibration, subtle like a subwoofer lying face down in shag carpet, was just enough to be picked up if they held their breath. Jacob found his own spot in the grass and dropped low, holding his rifle to his chest. He sat listening, feeling the moisture from the ground seep into his clothing. The rumble grew louder. Duke's posture became rigid, causing James to instinctively put an arm out for the dog and pull him close.

"Vehicles?" Jacob said.

"No, can't be. They'd get bogged down in the mud here," James whispered back.

With the thumping sound, the grass began to sway, slightly at first, then faster and more rhythmically. Rogers gazed back again, his eyes wide. He pointed two fingers at himself, and then stuck an index finger to the center of the valley, away from them on the opposite side just before the ground sloped up. Jacob pivoted then rose up on his knees to see. The rumble tickled at his ear drums, the vibration making the hair on the back of his neck buzz. Straining against the fading light, he saw them.

A column of … he didn't know what to call them. They were shoebox shaped and void of any solid color. The sides of the vehicles gave the impression of liquid metal that bent light and reflected the ground they traveled on. There were three in total, each identical, smoothly moving in a straight line, not hindered by the rough terrain. Behind the vehicles, a parade of Deltas followed in two disciplined columns. No longer armed, the black-eyed monsters marched standing straight up, evenly spaced apart.

"So that's how they do it," James whispered. "Hovercraft."

The vehicles appeared to float over the surface, the ground at the edges of the vehicles blowing outward with the beat of the rumbling subwoofer. Using a type of air displacement rather than conventional fans, they moved closer to the team on a course that would intersect with the small patrol.

From the top of the lead vehicle Jacob could clearly make out the body of an elongated man. The torso of the creature was long and narrow and wrapped in fabric that resembled blued steel. Its shoulders were padded in red ridged material, and the head covered in a helmet matching the shoulder pads. The creature was facing forward, its head swiveling from side to side.

Jacob, now fighting back fear, consciously struggled to control his shaking hands. He turned to look at James for an answer, surprised to see his friend hunched over the now unzipped canvas bag. Inside was a large scoped rifle. James went to work, quickly deploying the bipod and readying the scope while Rogers pushed rounds into a box magazine.

"What are you doing?" Jacob whispered, his voice breaking.

"Get the rocket off your back. The instructions are on the side; get familiar with them," Rogers answered in a tone letting Jacob know that now wasn't a time to hesitate.

James finished with the rifle and plucked the magazine from Rogers. Locking it in place, he put the stock in the ground, balancing the rifle while he dropped his pack and settled the bi-pod into it. Dropping low in a prone position, he tried to focus through the blowing grass.

"This won't be an easy shot, boss," he whispered, trying to hold the weight of the rifle as he racked a round into the chamber. Duke pnudged close to him and rested by James's side.

Rogers prepared his own AT4 for firing. "The one in the hatch is yours, James. Jacob, you have the middle vehicle. I'll take the trail vehicle and block them in," he said. "Shoot and scoot, easy money, that's all I'm asking. Anything we don't kill, James, you finish."

Rogers shifted away farther to the right then looked back at Jacob, who was looking down at the tube in his hands. "You having a problem?"

"What if the rockets don't work against them?"

"Only one way to find that out," Rogers said with a sly grin. "Just aim for the front of the vehicle; let the warhead do the worrying."

Jacob rested on his knees, his mind lulling behind in the action. He held the green tube in his hands, looking at the instructions but not comprehending any of it, the impending fight clouding and shocking his thoughts at the same time. Rogers crawled back beside him, moving behind James, who was already locked onto the creature exposed in the lead vehicle. Rogers handed Jacob the rocket he'd already prepped. Rogers put the rocket to Jacob's shoulder and pointed at the sight. "Too easy—look through the peep sight and squeeze this."

Jacob looked the weapon over and nodded, taking the full weight of the rocket in his hands while Rogers readied the next.

"I'm ready when you are," James whispered in their direction.

Rogers reached his left hand out and put up a thumb up to Jacob. "You start us off, Jake. Just give it a solid squeeze and hold steady; we're only a couple hundred yards out and they're at a crawl. Too easy."

Jacob held the tube on his right shoulder, steadying the AT4 with his left hand while his right thumb rested lightly on the trigger. He looked through the small peephole sight. The shoebox seemed to glow a phosphorous green, the shades of light shifting in browns and yellows as it moved over the uneven ground and vegetation. Focusing through the peep sight, he could now make out more detail within the active camouflage—the edges and contoured lines of the vehicle, hatches, and exhaust ports. The grass moved with the beat of whatever kept the vehicles in the air.

"Any time now," Rogers whispered.

Jacob swallowed hard and put the sight just to the front edge of the vehicle; he squeezed the safety and pushed the trigger. The blast of the rocket shattered his ears. He looked away just as he saw the shoebox erupt into flames. Rogers fired next to him, and James released a salvo from the heavy rifle in steady beats.

The large rifle roared, pushing grass away in the wake of every round. Jacob saw Rogers flip his expended rocket tube forward into the grass and raise up his rifle. Jacob shook off the shock and did the same. Looking through the sights of the M14, he could see the vehicles were different now. Burning hulks of dark brown, the luminescence died with whatever made it. Both vehicles hit by rockets were engulfed in flames. The alien convoy never had a chance.

The air was still, the rumbling vibrations now gone. The second vehicle was sitting idle, the mirrored image of the terrain flickering on its sides as James pumped armor-piercing rounds into it. The creature once exposed in the hatch was nearly gone, only a portion of its decapitated body still partially visible. Panning to the left he saw the Deltas still standing in their disciplined formation seemingly unaffected by the violence.

James fired the last round and quickly packaged the M82, shouting “up” as he finished to let Rogers know he was ready to move.

Rogers turned and pulled Jacob to his feet saying, “Let’s move. We need to get clear of here.” Jacob stumbled up and lunged forward. He looked back over his shoulder to the burning vehicles, the billowing smoke filling the sky.

With Duke close by his side, James hoisted the pack to his shoulders. “I’d like to take a closer look at those vehicles.”

Rogers shook his head and stepped off. “No time, who knows if they have communications or air cover? I don’t want to hang around and find out.”

Jacob drew his rifle close to his chest and dropped his head, picking up the pace to keep up with the other two. Rogers moved them back to the opposing wall of the valley, scrambling up a steep incline until they were hidden in a rocky embankment.

He fell into the cover of a downed tree and thick mud where rains had long ago caused a slide. The debris now formed a high earthen wall of tree trunks and stone. Jacob ducked behind them, crawling forward and turning so that his back was pressed against a tall rock. He looked up and saw James reloading the box magazine with .50 rounds while Rogers was back on his binoculars, looking out between two large boulders across the valley.

“What now?” Jacob gasped between labored breaths.

Rogers removed the binoculars from his eyes and sipped at a bottle of water. “The Deltas are still down there. Still in that stupid line.”

Duke began to growl, and the hair on the dog’s neck stiffened.

Jacob crawled next to Rogers amid the tall rocks and looked out. As he'd said, the Deltas were standing as still as statues, still in their columns facing the burning vehicles. "Wait … there! What's that?" Jacob whispered, pointing to movement in the tall grass beyond the burning vehicles.

Rogers adjusted his binoculars and swiveled in the direction Jacob indicated. "Aww, hell, the cavalry is here."

Jacob watched as the things smoothly glided through the tall grass, approaching from the high ground on the opposite end of the valley. Lean and elongated, their bodies were covered in blue steeled fabric with gold piping on the arms; heads that seemed disproportionately large for their bodies were covered by helmets. Each one carried a type of compact battle rifle that was held with two hands. They moved gracefully, taking long striding steps. Two in the back and one farther to the front, they approached the line of Deltas and looked up and down the column before moving close to inspect the burning convoy.

"I count three. We can take—" Before Rogers could finish, more came, moving swiftly through the tall grass. At a full run, their speed could challenge an African Gazelle.

"Make that ten," Jacob whispered.

Rogers used a flat hand to silence the exchange and leaned in. Jacob saw the things crowd around the vehicles. Even though alien, it was easy to read their body language. Their heads darted and they faced out in all directions. They were afraid. The creatures moved back to the column of Deltas, shoving and swatting at them violently with their rifles, forcing the column back on the move. Soon the column was marching again, the aliens' attention focused on the Deltas as they passed through the center of the valley.

"Look at the bastards. They should be patrolling the tree lines; instead, their eyes are glued on the black eyes. We should hit them again out of principle," James whispered. Jacob turned and saw him perched just over his shoulder.

"Why aren't they coming after us?" Jacob asked.

Rogers dropped his binoculars, the group close enough now to see them clearly. "I don't think they're soldiers. Yeah, they're armed, but look how they move; that's no formation, just a gaggle. These things aren't used to resistance."

"Well, something resisted. You heard that fight when we first got here," Jacob rebutted.

Rogers nodded. "You're right. Still, I'm surprised at how soft their vehicles were; they drove straight ahead, turrets unmanned."

"Maybe this is a logistics convoy," James said. "But wait, then that would mean … aww, shit."

Jacob looked back, alarmed. "It would mean what?"

"That we're behind enemy lines," Rogers said.

Chapter 6

Jacob sat motionless, watching another convoy roll across the valley floor. The light faded while the team lay low, forced to hold position in the rocks. The enemy activity increased all around them. Streams of alien vehicles filed into the valley. Unlike before, these new hovercraft had red-painted, armored turrets on the tops. Several vehicles were supported by ground troops. The alien infantry was different in appearance from the supporting troops Jacob saw earlier. The new creatures wore red, armored plates on their chest and back in addition to the blue, steel fabric. Tall and broad-chested, they were carrying large shoulder-fired weapons and shielded battle helmets. Walking stooped over forward, they moved tactically with their heads swiveling.

Jacob used a gloved hand to swat a bug from his chin, keeping his eyes glued to the enemy columns. "Where are they all going?" he whispered.

"Away from here," James answered. "From their posture, I'd say they're looking for a fight."

Rogers pushed away from the rocks and spun around. "My guess is south, toward our remaining strong points. Those columns are coming from the base. Landing parties … pushing troops out toward our lines … that's what I would do."

"We should get back to the cabin," Jacob whispered, watching Rogers nod in response.

James eased in between them and extended a hand in the air. "No, not yet."

"Why the hell not?" Jacob spat.

"Because look at them, they're loaded for bear. If they're headed toward the guys holding the lines, or even worse, the refugee camps … We have others to think about now; the civilians in the camps, the men ahead in the trenches—"

Rogers leaned forward and looked at both of the soldiers across from him. "We can't stop this, James."

"No, but we can try to slow them down, allow our boys to organize. We have an opportunity here. If we hit them hard, they'll be forced to put resources on us."

Jacob shook his head in frustration. "We don't know if there is anybody left *to* organize, and if we get ourselves killed? How does that help anyone?"

"Fuck it then, you two go, Duke and I got this," he said, running his hand down the dog's back.

"Can it, James, nobody is saying that. We just need to think, is all. Consider all the options," Rogers said. "Hide or fight … either way we need to be smart. If we hit them again, they'll certainly come after us, and if we hide, how long will it be before they find us?"

"We shouldn't be talking about this here; we need to get back to the cabin," Jacob said, pulling his pack toward him. "We should load up and take the Blackhawk back to Stone's place. If we want to fight them, we should do it from there, not here."

Suddenly, gunfire echoed across the valley. The men spun around and pressed back to the opening, Rogers squeezing between them with his binoculars in hand, searching the opposing high ground. On the far ridge line were muzzle flashes, tracers raining down into the alien soldiers. Rounds pinged and slapped into the soft earth around the convoy. A group of the red armor-clad infantry bounded ahead toward the ridge. Taking long leaps and landing with planted feet, they squatted and turned their rifles upward, opening fire as the vehicles' turrets rotated and unleashed a barrage of blue flame.

With the same *voomp, voomp, voomp* they'd heard before, the barrels released blue bolts of energy—something Jacob had never seen outside of a Hollywood movie. The bolts propelled forward, the blue energy sticking to and engulfing anything it made contact with in a bright blue flame. The noise of battle increased while the alien infantry and armored vehicles moved toward the ridge line. Soon all of their forces were engaged, the bright light of their weapons forcing Jacob's eyes away. The gunfire from the ridge lessened as whatever attacked was killed or withdrew over the ridge line.

Rogers backed away and grabbed at James's shoulder. "There will be time to fight later, let's go." The big man rolled then crawled away back toward the tower.

James twisted and leaned back into the rocks, the flashes of the battle reflecting off his face. He switched his gaze between Jacob and his leader then grimaced, knowing full well that they were out-gunned. He dipped his head in surrender and conceded they wouldn't win any fights tonight. James gathered his gear and followed Rogers into the night with Jacob close behind him, the flashes and *voomps* of the battle continuing at their backs.

Jacob followed them to the summit of the hill and rolled over the top. They came out farther away from the tower. Rogers gathered them without speaking and led them out, walking quietly with his weapon up. The rifle fire had stopped, but they could still hear the *voomps* of the enemy weapons, and bright flashes lit the sky to their backs.

Rogers led them over the side and down along the tower past the bunker entrance. He checked the lock then continued on down the trail without stopping. Jacob fell farther back, allowing James and Duke to take point as he lagged back into rear security. After a short distance, Rogers fell in beside him, checking both sides of the trail and looking at the illuminated dial on his watch.

"We'll get them out," he whispered.

Jacob nodded, understanding who he was talking about. "How?"

"We'll take the Blackhawk."

Jacob stalked several steps, scanning the dark path ahead and watching James's cautious movements. "What if they shoot it down?"

Rogers didn't answer. He held up a hand, pausing Jacob then pulling him down to the muddy trail. Ahead on the path, James vanished from sight. Jacob was alarmed he hadn't seen it; he didn't know where the point man went. He took the nudge, found the side of the trail, and dropped to a prone position with his rifle ahead of him. Looking right, he saw

Rogers doing the same, perched up on his elbows with his eyes just over the sights of his rifle and looking intensely into the dark.

To the left came a loud snapping of a branch and the shuffling of feet in the leaves. Jacob twisted, searching the thick vegetation for movement. A flicker of light appeared and a low voice sounded out, followed by a high-pitched voice that was lost and frustrated. "Joe, you don't know where the hell you're going."

"Shut up, they might be out here," responded a tall man.

Jacob held his rifle steady and dropped his head, waiting for a response from his leader. The men broke the thick vegetation and stumbled onto the trail. Moving into the open just ahead of Jacob, two men, both unarmed, stepped to the center of the trail that divided them from James. The men continued to argue as more people spilled into the clearing, crouching behind them. The others were silent, but from the silhouettes Jacob could tell they were women and children. Smaller in stature and not burdened with gear, they cast a thinner shadow.

He strained and looked across the trail to Rogers for a sign, seeing that his friend's head was down and slowly shaking from side to side. Jacob watched him remove a small pen light from his sleeve. He lifted it up and flashed the strangers with three quick splashes of green light before leaving the beam on and focused on the faces of the strangers.

The people on the trail froze; a gasp escaped the tall man's lips. He raised his right arm as his left palm reached out in an attempt to shield the light.

"Relax," Rogers said just above a whisper. "We're the good guys." Rogers cut the light, the transitions from bright to dark leaving the strangers on the trail momentarily blinded. "Who are you? Where are you going?"

The tall man lowered both arms and took a cautious step toward Rogers's voice. "We're just like you, trying to escape whatever is out there."

"You militia?" Rogers asked.

"What? No. We're from the village over the hill … well, what's left of it. I'm Clayton, this is my neighbor Ray." The man reached back and pointed to the smaller individual beside him.

"How many are you?"

"Ten—no …" The man paused. Jacob could see him put his head down and turn to the group behind him. "Six, mister. We're all that's left."

Jacob spotted James further up the trail; he'd circled back, keeping Duke close by his side and his rifle at the low ready. Rogers nodded to him, catching a mock salute in response.

"Okay, listen up. We don't have time for ice breakers and a get-to-know-ya. So let me make myself extremely clear. Stay quiet … no more talking … turn up the trail, follow my point man. Everyone is on edge and I don't want anyone getting hurt. I'll get you all to shelter; from there we can figure out what's what."

Chapter 7

Jacob followed the trail, keeping the civilians just ahead of him. Observing them, their awkward movements and noise ripped his thoughts back to his days before The Darkness. He would be in the same spot—or even worse—as these people if everything hadn't aligned for him. What at the time seemed like an incredible streak of bad luck, somehow kept his family alive. But alive for what? And how long?

Heavy clouds drifted in and blocked out the moon. Snowflakes began to fall with the dropping temperatures. The people ahead suddenly stopped. Jacob heard James whisper, calling Rogers forward. More muffled voices joined the conversation at the front of the column. He stepped off the trail and passed the others, making his way to the front. A stout man wearing an unzipped, camouflage parka over a thick, black fleece was standing next to James. More uniformed men just behind him quickly grabbed control of the civilians and led them up the trail to the block house and field with the Blackhawk.

"Looks like the cavalry has arrived," Jacob said.

His words caught the attention of the parka-clad man. The man's head turned and caught the pale moonlight, causing a thick scar to glisten. Jacob immediately recognized him.

"Masterson?" Jacob whispered.

James looked up and watched him approach, grinned, and then waved Jacob forward. Masterson shook his head watching Jacob move out of the darkness.

"Well, shit son! Anderson, you've outlived your expectations."

"Drill Serg—"

"You can cut that shit, it's Masterson now. I saw your buddy all busted up. You did well though, getting your woman and kid here."

"Laura. You saw them?"

Masterson raised a hand, covering a cough, and then removed a canteen from his hip and brought it to his lips. Jacob noticed the burns on the man's neck and hands. "I moved everyone up here to the block house. It's not safe farther down the trail; it's too close to the road. Their patrols are picking up."

"Patrols?"

A second man with a heavily grayed beard, dressed in a well-worn canvas coat and faded jeans, moved in from the shadows and asked, "Who's this you found?"

Masterson clenched his jaw, returning the canteen to its carrier. "Anderson, meet Clem. Clem, this guy here is one of our recent graduates."

"Any good, is he?" the bearded man asked.

Masterson grinned. "He ain't dead yet, so good 'nuff."

Jacob shook his head and stepped closer. "I'm right here, you know. So what about these patrols?"

Masterson grunted and fished a can of tobacco from a breast pocket. He stuffed a wad in his cheek then looked around before continuing in a low voice. "Yeah, they're spreading out fast. Not sure what the hell is going on, but we had to get away from the road. Further back, and into heavier trees we get, the better. So far they stick close to those floating APCs."

"We hit a small group in the valley about a mile due east of here."

Masterson's eyes narrowed as he eyed up at Jacob. "Yellow or red?"

Jacob squinted, not understanding the question.

"Their armor, was it yellow or red?"

Duke whined restlessly and James sighed, stepping away from the end of the trail he was guarding, and interrupted. "Let's move this conversation inside. It's not safe out here in the open."

Rogers, along with most of the civilians, had already moved on and entered the small block house, leaving the rest of them alone in the dark. A small gathering of soldiers was standing sentry in the field near the lone helicopter while others patrolled closer to the block building.

Masterson nodded his agreement and moved out of the way, waving his hand toward the house. James stepped off, leading the way with Jacob close behind him. The door to the blockhouse hung open. A thick tarp was draped over the opening to block the light inside from escaping. Jacob pulled back the tarp and stepped into the warm interior.

He immediately felt the heat of the wood fire and smelled the savory scent of roasted meat and vegetables. At the front of the crowded low-lit building, people were sitting at two long picnic tables. Jacob stepped deeper into the space, feeling the crunch of dried leaves under his boots. He could see the strangers from the trail were already working on bowls filled with stew. Huddled around low burning candles that were randomly positioned over the plank tables, they ate quietly while being mindful of the soldiers lying in sleeping bags at the back of the house.

Jacob let his eyes scan the place until he saw them—Laura and Katy in a makeshift kitchen along a side wall. Katy sat in a tall chair while Laura helped Buck, their pilot, fill bowls with stew.

Jacob followed his stomach and moved off in their direction before being caught by the sleeve. He turned back to see Masterson looking back at him. "I know you're eager to get off duty, but let's get this out of the way first. Tell me about them … the ones you hit in the valley."

Rogers crept up from the dark with bowls in his hands. "What about it?" he said.

"Who were they?" Masterson asked.

Rogers passed a bowl to Jacob then pointed to an empty place at the table. Jacob nodded and dropped onto a bench seat beside him. "They were a type of support troops, riding tall and dumb with no cover. We took out three of those invisible cars. They were soft … unarmed from what I could see. Our AT4s and the fifty cut through them like butter."

As the men talked, Jacob watched Laura work in the kitchen, returning items to their place and chatting with the other women. She turned away from a stove and made eye contact with Jacob, casting him a knowing smile before turning back to finish.

"What about reinforcements?" Masterson asked, forcing Jacob to look back across the table at the scarred man.

Rogers scooped another spoonful of the stew before continuing for him. "A group of others responded, gold shirts, yellow sleeves. Later, some heavies showed up. They were different, bigger. Blue uniforms with red chest plates, heavier rifles. Then more vehicles with red turrets—probably their version of a quick reaction force. We were planning to let them pass,"—Rogers shook his head—"but some unit on the far side of the valley engaged them—"

Masterson frowned and cut him off with a loud sigh. "Echo Company," he said. "Explains the gunfire we heard and why they missed the rendezvous. We traveled separate. We went south of the road, Echo north. I figure that would have put them in the spot you're talking about."

Rogers finished the stew and pushed the bowl away from him, wiping his face with his sleeve. "They put up a fight, but it didn't do no good. Those things opened up with some big guns, crazy shit like we've never seen before. Last glimpse I got, they were chasing them toward Meaford."

"Doesn't surprise me; The Colonel was always itching for a fight," Clem added.

"Who?" Jacob asked.

Masterson used a chunk of bread to catch the last of his stew. "Our battalion commander; solid officer and good guy. He's in charge of all the training companies. I know he's been looking for a fight since they relieved him off the line and put him in charge of training."

"How many did he have with him?" Rogers asked.

"Not many. Forty … maybe fifty trainees, another dozen instructors. Hell, we're all that's left. Only thing that spared us from the bombing is that we were far enough from the main base when they dropped that shit. Colonel Grady rode out with the training company. I had most of the support guys and half the instructors. We ran into a small group of the base security forces, and they told us about you all making it for the outpost, so we joined up with them and moved out."

Rogers shook his head slowly, understanding. "Any other survivors?"

“’Fraid not, the base is a total loss. I plan to move back down the road toward friendly lines tomorrow. See if we can find a safe place. I’m going to need some of your scouts,” Masterson said.

“There’s no scouts. Counting Jesse with his neck wound, there are only four of us that made it out.”

Masterson rubbed at the stubble on his chin and looked at the three tired men across from him. “Then, I guess you’re it. Be ready to move at first light.”

Chapter 8

It was impossible for him to sleep with the gunfire and explosions rumbling like a distant thunderstorm. Roaring concussions rattled the roof and windows of the small block house. The enemy—the things—were getting closer. His mind screamed for him to grab his family and run, but he knew he couldn't; they would never survive alone.

Jacob lay awake; he tossed and turned then flipped onto his back hard before pulling the heavy blanket from his chest. He rolled off of the makeshift sleeping mat and pushed up to a seated position, leaning against the wall. His mind raced with thoughts of despair and dread. If this really was an alien invasion, how would they ever last the winter?

Katy and Laura remained soundly asleep beside him, nestled against the wall under heavy blankets. A low glow from the woodstove in the corner emitted the only light. Men snored away; a soldier by the front entrance stood watch, and Jacob watched the man fill a tin cup from a blue coffee pot.

"They're fighting again," Laura whispered.

Jacob turned to look down at her, putting his hand on her shoulder as he nodded his reply.

"How long has it been going on?" she asked.

Another distant impact shook the rafters. "Couple of hours, maybe … Don't worry, it's not close." Jacob put his head back and looked at the ceiling. "The cloud cover and valley just make it seem like it."

"You're going back out, aren't you?"

He forced a smile and nodded as his hand squeezed her shoulder. She moved closer, letting her head rest in his lap. Jacob could see the swelling in her eyes, knowing she had cried when the stories of the base's destruction sped through their meager camp. He dropped his arms on her shoulders and felt her trembling.

"I'll go if they'll take me. This isn't like before; we have to stay ahead of them to survive."

Laura moved, reaching up to grasp his hands. "Why do you have to go?"

He sighed, squeezing her hands. "This isn't something we can hide from."

She turned her head to look up at him but didn't speak, and she closed her eyes while pulling his hands to her cheeks.

"We're going to have a look around. I'll be back then we can leave and find some place safe," Jacob whispered.

"I know you'll be fine. I just want us to be together."

***

Before the others woke, Jacob followed the men out of the block house and into the cold morning air. He felt the near freezing temperatures bite at his neck and pulled up the collar of his shirt. He caught a whiff of cigarette smoke mixed with the brisk morning air. Turning his head, he saw Buck with a wool blanket over his shoulders, a smoke in one hand, and a thermos cup in the other while Masterson and Rogers crowded around him.

"Have the bird prepped and ready when we get back," Masterson told him in a matter-of-fact tone.

Buck nodded his head slowly and smiled, showing his stained teeth. "She'll be ready." Buck paused and looked left and right before stepping closer and lowering his voice. "I can only take ten. You'll have some decisions to make."

Masterson grimaced then returned the pilot's smile. "Multiple trips then; I'm sure you're up for it."

Buck shrugged. "Assuming we have fuel to top off the tanks for a second trip, and what about security?"

Masterson looked back and caught Jacob listening in on the conversation; he brought up a gloved hand and slapped Buck's cloaked shoulder. "Let the gunfighters worry about that; just be ready to go."

Masterson stepped into the clearing near the helicopter and waved his arms, bringing the twenty-man patrol into a tight cluster. The plan for them was to move back down the trail to the cabin and barn then meet the dirt access road. If all remained clear, they would move over it and into nearby hills. Once on high ground, they could set up a hide position so that they could observe the main road and intersections.

Most of the soldiers in Masterson's party were veterans and knew the part they would play. Experienced, they had performed these drills countless times on foreign battle fields. But today, everyone was wary. Even though the noise of the distant battles had dropped off with the rising of the sun, the men still didn't know what to expect. This wasn't Afghanistan or Iraq where everyone played a role; nobody knew what to expect from this new brand of invaders, or even what purpose the Deltas would have in everything.

"Don't get too heavy on your triggers; we have half of a missing company out there and who knows what else. Stay quiet and keep this place a secret as long as we can." With that, Masterson ended his conversation and pointed to Rogers.

Rogers took a deep breath and dipped his chin. "A'right, let's get this done. James, you got point. Jacob, take slack with me."

Jacob found his spot in the file and patroled cautiously with his rifle in the crook of his elbow, his gloved right hand resting on the stock. They packed light for the patrol; no heavy rucksacks or body armor to weigh them down. Most of them didn't have armor anyway, and who knew if it was effective against the invaders' weapons? Nobody had been able to examine a dead alien—or even one of their victims for that matter.

James waved a hand to the ground, slowing them as they approached the main cabin. The place appeared empty; a low fog hung close to the structures and blanketed the lonely buildings. In the yard of the cabin, Jacob spotted the trucks they used to get there. Along with their trucks were several open-backed Humvees and a massive cargo truck, and a white Toyota pickup was next to the barn. James let Duke move on his own, the dog zigzagging between the vehicles and stopping to sniff the air.

The point man knelt near a tree, waiting for the dog to return before he waved the others forward. Jacob moved close and squatted, finding a position where he could watch the road. He heard Masterson order five of the men to stay and secure the cabin site before ordering Rogers to push ahead. As Jacob got back to his feet, he could feel the mood change. The hair on his neck buzzed with electricity; moving onto the road felt dangerous and foreign to him.

Looking back at Rogers's stone face and clenched jaw, he knew his leader was feeling it too. They were in a dangerous place now. James moved them across the road and onto high ground on the far side. It was a low ridge that gave them viewpoints over the gravel access road. They turned and moved south, cutting through a saddle and onto a high tree-covered slope. Working their way to the top, they could begin to see the shapes of roofs and far off buildings from the high vantage point.

Pillars of black smoke snaked up from a bunching of homes. Farther away, where the gravel road met the paved highway, was a cluster of destroyed and smoldering vehicles—civilian cars and military trucks twisted and smashed. The distance spared him some of the carnage, but Jacob knew what he would find if he wandered closer.

James dropped into the cover of a large tree and waited for his teammates to join him. He huddled the dog close to his side, pointed down at the destroyed vehicles, and said, “What’s left of last night’s battle.”

Jacob used the scope on the M14 to examine the devastation. Nothing moved; no signs of life. Panning from left to right, he could see more signs of black smoke on the horizon. The rest of Masterson’s men moved up behind him and formed a wide half-circular perimeter on the face of the hill. Riflemen moved in with nervous anticipation, finding bits of cover and concealment as they searched the far off sights.

Clem, the rough and tattered civilian, weaved in close to James with Masterson right behind him. He retrieved a pair of olive-green binoculars from his hip pocket and scanned the distant horizon. He pointed his hand and waved it past the distant streams of black smoke. “They’re hitting every bit of civilization between here and Lake Huron.”

Rogers ignored the older man. “We should go down and have a look, check for survivors.”

Clem pivoted and pointed to the east. The road twisted and disappeared into a series of deep cuts and rolling hills scattered with heavy trees. "No, they're close; we need to stay out of sight."

Rogers shook his head. "How the hell do you know that?"

"Cause it's war. The sides change but tactics are always relative." Clem paused to look down at the twisted, smoldering vehicles. "Looks like local survivors trying to make a caravan west away from the landings. Got ambushed just past the intersection and tried to push through. Military escort pulled up ahead and went down with 'em.

"Yeah … if it was me, I'd have shot up everything in the kill box down there then dropped back into the cover of those hills. Yeah, I reckon they're waiting in there."

Rogers looked at Masterson with a smirk. "Who the hell is this guy?"

Clem put up a flat hand, waving off the comment. "I'm a nobody, kid, don't you worry about me," he said, passing the binoculars to Masterson.

The scarred soldier took the glasses and opened his mouth to speak when Clem raised his hand, silencing him. "Listen," he said.

Rogers rolled his eyes. “What now, old timer?”

Clem pointed to the sky and looked at the tree tops. Slowly, the sound of helicopter blades beating came into range just before a pair of Apaches tore over their heads, so close to the treetops, they knocked snow off the high branches. Following the terrain, they dropped in elevation then banked hard into a gun run over the nestled crop of hills Clem had pointed out earlier. Without slowing, the attack helicopters let loose a salvo of hydra rockets. Bright streams of white disappeared into the hills. The sounds of thundering explosions echoed back as it mixed with the belching of the helicopters’ 30mm guns.

Blue streaks reached up into the sky after the Apaches, harmlessly falling far off course. The helicopters banked hard and made a second high-speed pass, launching Hellfire missiles before climbing and disappearing. The enemy fire ceased, the cluster of hills now engulfed in fire and smoke. Secondary explosions snapped and popped from the cluster of hills as the sounds of the Apaches faded. Jacob looked down and could see the men on the hilltop perch up with excitement on their faces.

“Well, I’ll be … our birds can kill them,” Clem said.

"Who are they?" Jacob asked.

"Pelee. They must be out of Pelee Island. They're the only ones with attack birds left," Masterson said.

Jacob grabbed his pack and started to stand. "Then that's where we'll go. The airspace must be clear; the Blackhawk could get through … right?"

Rogers shook his head. "No. Whatever these things are, they'll be going after them now."

Jacob turned to face him. "How? You saw the helicopters … those shots didn't even come close. They don't have air defense."

"You may be right, but I don't like assumptions. We'll use the diversion of the Apache strike to get our own people back to the bunker."

Clem grabbed a handful of dirty snow and squeezed it in his fist. "He's right. They'll focus on those attack birds. Start moving whatever they have after them to pinpoint the source. We can move away from it. Take advantage of the vacuum."

Masterson climbed to his feet, lifting his rifle with him. "Okay, I like it." He pointed a finger at a nearby soldier and called him close. "Send two of your people back to the compound. Tell that pilot to ferry the first batch out."

The young soldier turned to run away when Masterson grabbed his shoulder. “Make sure that old bastard knows to turn around and come straight back, and tell him I don’t care if he returns on fumes.”

“Yes, Master Sergeant,” the man said over his shoulder as he rushed off.

Jacob watched impatiently as a pair of men accepted their instructions and moved back down the hill. He looked up at Masterson and grabbed his sleeve. “What the hell are we still doing up here?”

Masterson smiled. “Our day ain’t done. I want to take a peek in them hills.”

Chapter 9

The point man and his dog stealthily rose up and approached the steep slope angling down to the intersection. "I'll lead us out," James whispered.

"Stay close to him," Rogers said, leaning in to Jacob so the others couldn't hear. "I don't like the looks of this."

Jacob filed down the hill, keeping James to his front. As he moved he watched the rest of the patrol step up and file in behind them, slowly joining the column. James led them down the face of the hill and pushed up against the hard-packed shoulder of the road. He knelt into cover, causing the rest of the men to follow his lead. Jacob crouched in the heavy grass and weeds, feeling the cold snow press against his clothing.

They lay silent, becoming one with the terrain while James and Duke strained their ears to listen for any sign of danger at the side of the road. It was beyond quiet, nothing moved; the leaves even seemed to freeze on their limbs. Down the road to the left, he could see the doomed civilian caravan; to the right, an open road leading back to the base and the neighboring villages. The air reeked with the stench of burnt rubber and plastics mixed with death. Rogers crept up behind Jacob and again whispered, "I don't like it."

"Do you see something?" Jacob asked.

"No, but it shouldn't be this quiet. If we were alone, you'd hear the animals … birds or something; even the damn bugs are hiding."

After a long fifteen minutes, James rushed across the road, cutting a path through the fresh snow. Rogers pointed it out as they followed it. "Everything about this is wrong," he whispered. The rest of the men quietly rose to their feet and fell in behind them. Jacob picked up his pace, letting Rogers tuck in behind him as he crossed the open roadway. Soon he was wading back into the thick foliage on the other side. At the base of the hill, the vegetation was thick as it wrapped around him, making it nearly impossible to see. He moved ahead, following James by sound alone.

This is bad, I can't see shit, Jacob thought. He used his left hand to push thick brush aside as he navigated the thick underbrush. It was impossible to stay quiet; the branches and thorns grabbed at his clothing, scratching any exposed skin. It was darker and colder at the bottom of the hill, and the smoke seemed to build up and blanket the ground. Jacob could taste it now. The thick, acrid, metallic taste burned at the roof of his mouth, causing his nose to run.

James led them through the slight depression then up into another rising hill. The vegetation became sparser and allowed Jacob to open his stride. The hilltop cleared and opened into a mound of yellow grass.

Near the summit, James dropped to a crouch and slowly backed himself up before he lowered his body to the ground. He rolled to his back and waved Jacob forward. Jacob did as instructed, dropping to his belly and leopard crawling ahead while holding up the muzzle of his rifle as he crept to the front. He moved up to just beside James's thighs, Duke leaning down to greet him with a lick to his face. The dog scampered slowly in a circle and dropped into the grass with a sigh.

Jacob waited for Rogers to join them before he rotated to his hip and looked up at James. The point man rolled onto his back, gazing up at the clear blue sky partially obscured by the blooms of black acrid smoke. Now closer, Jacob could hear the occasional pops and snaps of burning wood and parts of the alien vehicles.

“You get eyes on them?” Rogers asked.

James looked into their faces and spoke in a hushed tone. “On the other side … down the center of a wide road.”

“Numbers?” Rogers whispered.

James shook his head side to side. “Hard to tell; Apaches fucked ’em up. I didn’t see any moving, but I didn’t hang out long either.” He struggled with his equipment, pulling a canteen from his hip. James took a long drink before pouring more into his palm and offering it to Duke. “We shouldn’t be here … this is the kind of shit that gets people killed,” he said. “They’ll be moving in to collect on their dead, and to collect our heads.”

Rogers opened his mouth to speak but held his tongue when he heard Clem and Masterson moving up behind them. The scarred man moved in close and glared at all of them. “Why are we stopped?” he asked impatiently.

“They’re just over the top,” James answered. “It’s not secure.”

Masterson grinned and rolled to his back before sitting up. He held his arms straight out and waved them up and down, signaling for his men to get on line. He dropped his gear and crawled ahead, pushing Jacob aside as he forced his way next to

James. “Okay, we’ll cover you from up here while you all go down and check it out.”

“Fuck that! I ain’t doing nothing of the sort. You want to go down and say hello then have at it,” James retorted.

Masterson’s jaw clenched. He reached out a hand and grabbed the shoulder of James’s jacket. Clem chuckled from behind them. “If your boy is scared, I can go down myself,” the old man said.

Before Masterson could respond, there was a loud clanking of metal. James put up a hand, silencing both of them as he rolled back to his belly and crawled to the top of the hill. Not waiting for instruction, Jacob did the same, edging forward through the high grass. The snow was lighter here; in direct sunlight, most of it had already melted off.

Looking ahead, Jacob could see that the grass continued over the top of the hill then dropped swiftly down to meet the paved road on the far side. Stretching down the middle of the roadway was a column of destroyed and burning alien vehicles, black smoke boiling from the wreckage. He was surprised to see Rogers moving ahead of them; ducking down, he bear-crawled on all fours and waded into the thick grass, only his head and shoulders showing.

The rest of the men fanned out and followed his lead while Jacob stood in a crouched stance. He felt Duke brush against his side; the dog was still relaxed, its tail wagging feverishly. Jacob tried to let the dog's temperament comfort him, Duke always being a fair gauge for danger.

Jacob paused in his movements and held his rifle's optic to his eye, panning down the long roadway. He counted at least six of the destroyed hovercrafts, all burning, some brighter than others, the metal putting off strobe-like flashes of light similar to burning magnesium. Where the vehicle occupants tried to escape the inferno, there were charred bodies in the road. Jacob looked back and saw the patrol's riflemen now lining the top of the hill; some knelt down, others stood. If they were shocked, their faces hid it well. The men were stoic, weapons out providing over watch.

James stepped closer. He raised his rifle up and held it steady with his right hand while he pointed to a still body with his left. "This one's still got all its parts. This what you're looking for?"

Clem hissed and halted the others as he alone approached the blue-clad figure. The old man stepped beside it and nudged the body with his boot, getting no response. He leaned down and pulled the form over, its lifeless, helmeted head flopping to the side. It was one of the Yellow Sleeves, smaller than the Reds.

"Thing fuckin' stinks, don't it?"

Clem pushed at the thing's chest with the stock of his rifle, the figure contorting with the pressure.

"Freeze!" James hissed, holding up a flat hand.

Clem stopped cold, his body instinctively crouching at the warning. "What is it?"

Jacob turned on his heels to look back at his friend. He saw Duke with his back arched, lips curled back revealing white fangs, a low growl slowly rising in volume. James was by the dog's side, his rifle at the low ready, trying to follow the dog's intense gaze.

"We're not alone down here," James whispered. "We need to move."

A dry heat suddenly filled the air. Blue bolts of energy rushed at them from all directions. Jacob dove for the soft earth at the edge of the burning vehicles, hearing the sounds of the patrol returning fire from the hillside. Machine guns and deafening explosions joined the now familiar metallic *voomp* of the enemy weapons. He felt the tickling vibration in his ears and knew the alien vehicles were on the move. Fighting to his knees, he searched and spotted the first of the enemy hovercraft emerging from the far tree lines, their red turrets glowing as blue bolts raced in his direction.

"*Cover!*" Clem screamed.

Rogers reached down and yanked Jacob to his feet, pulling and nearly throwing him into the high grass as men above tossed smoke and tear gas canisters, desperately attempting to conceal their withdrawal. Jacob lunged at the hillside, falling and grabbing at the thick grass while scrambling up the steep slope.

"Pull back! Get to the woods," Masterson shouted over the fighting.

Jacob lunged ahead, moving past Clem. The older man had dropped to his knees, howling "Don't stop. Keep moving" as he bled off a full magazine from his rifle.

Earth exploded near Jacob's face as blue vapor mixed with searing hot mud, the heat flashing against his exposed skin. Jacob looked away and clawed at the grass, following the report of the platoon's rifles toward friendly lines. He crested the hill just as another blast of blue caught a trooper square in the chest. The man flipped backward, a dark smoldering impression burning into the man's uniform. Jacob reached for him then pulled back in horror, seeing the damage the weapon caused—the blue plasma sticking and burning through flesh as it dripped from the soldier's ribs, consuming his organs.

"Oh God," he gasped.

Jacob forced himself away, following the others as they crawled for the concealment of the thick woods. Blue bolts arced over their heads, impacting with the treetops and showering them with burning debris. Jacob struggled on, the shouting and screams of agony mixing with the *voomps* of the enemy weapons. The now downward slope of the hill increasing his momentum, he followed the others crashing into the heavy brush. The men of the hilltop were now in a full retreat. Friendly gunfire ceased, the noise quickly replaced with the scent of spent rounds and a strange, charred, electrical stench.

Vegetation wrapped him like a thick blanket, giving a false sense of security as he fought his way forward. Lungs burning with every step, he sprinted down the hill to the next road. He could hear men crying out in pain ahead of him. He burst into an opening in the thicket, nearly falling on medics fighting to restrain a large soldier. Jacob recognized the wounded man as one of the unit's machine gunners.

The man's left arm was covered in the blue smoldering plasma. It sizzled and ate at his flesh, the skin and muscle appearing to melt and mix with it. The man's arm flailed as medics wrestled him while others worked to cover the plasma with dirt and pouring the contents of their canteens on the wound in feeble attempts to smother and neutralize the strange blue flame.

Clem rushed into the space from behind and stole a quick glance at the wound. He drew a long knife from his belt and passed it to a medic. "Get that arm off him … now."

The husky soldier struggled and attempted to right himself, pleading with them not to take his arm. "I'll be okay, just wrap it up," he gasped.

Clem dropped to the ground and pressed his face close to the injured man. "You need to suck it up," he snarled through gritted teeth. "You're giving away our fuckin position, now bite down." Clem stuffed a handful of folded cloth in the man's teeth. The soldier's eyes clenched tight, sweat building on his forehead, tears breaking from the corners of his eyes. He chomped down and growled.

A young medic who'd already applied a field tourniquet above the wound, rested on his knees. Holding the blade in his shaking hand, he looked up at Clem with a deep worried expression and said, "I don't have anything for his pain."

"Then do it quick," Clem said in a matter-of-fact tone before leaving the clearing, pushing Jacob and the others ahead of him.

Jacob picked up on Duke's panicked bark and the echoes of snapping branches. He moved to the sound in a hurry. At the bottom of the decline, he lost his footing and tumbled through the thick vines and thorny bushes. Falling face first, he broke from the trees and plummeted into a low ditch at the side of the road. Water from the melting snow splashed his face and snapped him back. He rolled to his back and scooted up to the roadside, once again facing the doomed civilian convoy. A soldier already on his feet hooked an arm under his shoulder and pulled Jacob up from the ground. "Sergeant, we need to get off the road."

He resisted the soldier's grasp, suddenly embarrassed by the momentary loss of conscious thought. Jacob stood and held his rifle to his chest, taking deep breaths and pushing the shock from his mind.

"Sergeant, what do we do?"

Jacob stood stunned, not realizing the soldier was speaking to him.

"Sergeant?" the young soldier asked again.

Jacob shook his head and squeezed his eyes tight before looking back at the soldier. "Get everyone together; we'll be moving soon." He spotted Rogers standing on the road and quickly rushed to his leader's side. Rogers was pointing down the road in the direction of the cabin.

Jacob felt his blood run cold when he spotted the thin stream of black smoke. "No …"

Chapter 10

Laura pulled the straps tight on the nylon backpack. "I think we have everything. Now we just wait for Daddy to get back," she said, smiling down at her daughter beside her.

"And Duke," the girl replied.

"Yes, and Duke." Laura laughed, pulling Katy in for a hug. She hoisted the pack to her shoulders and gripped the M4 rifle in her left hand. Looking down at Katy, the girl grinned and reached up to her. She gripped Katy's hand and walked through the cramped space of the block house and out into the cool morning air.

Laura had never visited a place like this before. Some stops at manicured resort camp grounds, where they would rent a well-furnished condo on the lake shore, maybe a night in a friend's beach house, but nothing as sparse as this. Camping was Jacob's thing, a sentimental connection to his father, reminders of fishing trips they took together when he was a boy. Jacob tried to pass the same lessons on to Katy. "No daughter of mine will have to depend on a man to bait her hook," he used to joke.

She moved into the sunlight and watched the soldiers actively prepping the helicopter. The old man in the cowboy hat was fussing with them as they loosened ropes and readied equipment. Other people, refugees who came in with the soldiers, were sitting impatiently waiting; some argued with the soldiers and pointed at them accusingly.

The news of their departure to a possible safe area at first caused excitement, but when rumors spread that there wouldn't be enough room for everyone on the first flight, fights and heated discussions broke out. Everyone became suspicious of how the lucky passengers would be picked. Families of the soldiers, then women and children seemed the obvious choice, but families didn't want to be separated. And there wouldn't be seats for everyone.

A soldier with a notepad looked directly at Laura; he'd already stopped to talk to her earlier that morning. "Ma'am, I really think you and the little one should be on the first flight. As Sergeant Anderson's family, you have priority." A year ago, Laura would have never thought of speaking to a soldier—or even meeting one for that matter. Growing up in the suburbs of Chicago, the closest she ever got to the military was a local parade, or a patriotic TV commercial. Now, they came to her like she was part of the family, each of the soldiers feeling a responsibility to look after her.

Laura looked past him to the others—the refugees that stared at her suspiciously. They eyeballed her rifle, her backpack, even her boots. She knew they had nothing; they'd left everything behind, and she could easily be in the same position if things played out differently. She looked up at the soldier and shook her head no. "We won't leave until my husband returns," she said.

A man she recognized, husky with a bloodied bandage still clinging to his neck, moved past the others and stepped between her and the soldier. He frowned and leaned in close. "Ma'am, please, we heard gunfire down the road." Jesse paused and lowered his voice so the others couldn't hear. "There might not be a second flight. I owe it to Jacob to make sure you get on board."

"Not without my husband."

Gunshots echoed in the distance, causing them to look off to the east. Jesse dropped his gaze, not making eye contact while he spoke in a hushed tone. "Okay, but I have … well, I feel I have a responsibility to tell you … if they come … Mrs. Anderson, we won't be able to stop them."

Laura gave him a reassuring smile and put a hand on his forearm. "It's okay, Jesse. Let one of them have our spot. We'll be fine."

She led Katy away to a quiet spot farther from the helicopters and the soldiers. She set her pack on the ground and sat atop it while Katy kicked at the leaves and tossed small pine cones. Laura watched the soldiers selecting a young woman holding an infant from the group. The woman looked in Laura's direction and waved as she was led to the waiting helicopter. Katy stood close to her mother's side and returned the woman's wave.

"Momma, look, the baby is going on a helicopter," she said.

Laura pursed her lips and nodded, already feeling a tear form in the corner of her eye, wondering if she was making the wrong decision. She watched the soldiers make a final pass around the helicopter. They gave the old man a thumbs up then stepped away. The man removed his hat and moved into the Blackhawk. The turbine whined and the blades began to rotate.

The spinning of the blades increased; Laura leaned over, pulling Katy in to shield her from the wind. Soldiers moved around her, gathering in a cluster as debris began to blow, the Blackhawk fighting against gravity to leave the ground. The helicopter slowly lifted away, the tree tops swaying away from the blast of its rotors. Shielding the wind away with her hand, Laura looked up. She watched as the aircraft's nose dipped and, gaining altitude, slowly moved away.

Her stomach dropped, and her muscles constricted. Four thick bolts of blue arced up from nowhere. Time slowed as she watched them drift through the sky. The pilot must have spotted them; the helicopter banked hard to its right, dipping precariously close to the treetops. Three of the bolts arced high, missing it; the Blackhawk's nose dipped and the aircraft rotated clockwise before thrusting forward in the opposite direction. The third bolt scraped across the tail-rotor, launching the helicopter into a violent spin. The Blackhawk's turbines screamed for power as the pilot struggled for control.

Laura wanted to look away, but her eyes were glued to the sight. The helicopter tipped back, nearly inverted, before falling to the far end of the grassy field in a ball of orange and yellow flame. The force of the explosion and the heat from the burning fuel pulled her back, Katy still tight in her arms. She tumbled back, landing heavily in the thick grass.

Before she could open her eyes to recover, a soldier with stripes on his helmet was beside her, lifting her back to her feet. Finally her head cleared, and she heard yelling. Men were running among the scattered group, trying to direct the fight. "Get back, get back. Get the civilians to the woods, everyone else form on me," she heard the man with the stripes order.

The pack was gone. Katy, clinging to Laura's chest and arms locked around her neck, began to cry. Laura tried to lift her arms, realizing she was still holding the rifle in her left hand. Jesse swooped up her nylon backpack and steadied her. "Please, ma'am, we need to go," Jesse shouted, ushering her ahead.

Still stunned, she stepped back, Katy's screams clouding her thoughts. She stumbled for balance. The surrounding soldiers' weapons were firing, and the refugees screaming—some running to the block house; others aimlessly into the woods. Blue streaks of light raced across the field to her front.

"Ma'am," Jesse yelled, his face now inches from hers.

Laura swallowed hard and nodded. "Okay, let's go," she said in a dazed expression. Not afraid, she wondered, *Is this what shock feels like?*

Jesse forced a smile and led her forward. A bright flash of blue turned Laura's head in time to see a running man's body engulfed in a splash of blue. It looked like he'd been swallowed by illuminated jellyfish. *How beautiful,* Laura thought for a split second before the man's body was again revealed, nearly naked and stripped to the bone by the blue blaze.

"Oh shit," a crouched soldier shouted, looking down at the maimed man. He raised his rifle and fired at unseen targets to Laura's rear. She pushed forward, adrenaline spiking her senses, heart beating frantically, and Katy's tight grip around her neck. With clarity came the fear—she was now eager to escape. She ran the trail, struggling to keep up with the retreating soldiers and civilians ahead of her. They rounded a corner near a row of tiny cabins. Jesse stopped her with a tug at her elbow and pointed deeper into the woods to the north. Civilians ahead of her continued down the trail, others rushed through the thick vegetation in the direction Jesse indicated.

"Keep going, and don't stop. We'll hold them here," Jesse said.

"Where do I go?"

"Just run. Run until you can't hear the fighting, and then hide."

Laura hesitated, gunfire thundering in the distance. She pleaded with Jesse to go with her, to show her the way. He gave her a knowing nod and strapped the nylon backpack to her shoulders. He snatched her rifle and checked the action before placing it back into Laura's hands. "Go, stay quiet, and hide. We'll find you—Jacob will find you," he said solemnly, turning away. She went to follow in his direction when a blue bolt of energy splashed against one of the small cabins. The roughhewn pine boards were quickly swallowed in flame.

She looked back and saw that he'd been hit. The thigh of his uniform now scorched and blackened, somehow the big man managed to stay on his feet. He fired his rifle directly into the advancing enemy, not stopping until the bolt locked back. He shot her a scornful look as he reloaded. "Go," he yelled. "Get the hell out of here."

Katy screamed into her neck as she turned and followed the others into the trees.

Chapter 11

A distant groan of fire and earth rolled through the forest, the trembling ground forcing the soldiers of the beleaguered patrol to huddle together, their stomachs gripped tightly with fear. Looking in the direction of the camp, watching as the tiny pillar of black smoke was joined by a ball of orange flame and boiling black smoke, Jacob froze. His heart stopped as the men in Jacob's company lost any momentum they thought they'd earned from the helicopter attack.

"No, it can't be," he whispered.

Clem burst from the tree line, his oilskin coat now smeared with blood. He looked to the fight in the distance then back to the men, shoving them out of the clearing in the road and toward the cover of the forest. "Keep moving, get into the thick of it, we can lose them in the back country," he shouted. "We move south, away from it all."

Jacob stumbled back from the paralyzing fear. Looking over his shoulder at the older man who was still shouting orders, Jacob thought he caught a glimpse of a smile on the man's face—an eagerness for the man to be in charge, to take command, like he'd found his opportunity.

"We can't. We have to get back for my family … for the others … there could be survivors," Jacob said.

Men were already moving into the woods, vanishing in the thick trees like they'd been instructed. Masterson rushed ahead, passing a cluster of men and closed the distance, stepping between Jacob and the older man. "Clem, I appreciate your help, but you're not in charge here."

"Fuck who's in charge. I'm just trying to keep you lot alive. Soon, everyone at that campsite will be dead, and whatever is there will come back at us. Then we'll be sandwiched between them and the things just over the hill we're already running from."

Rogers stepped up next to James and cleared his throat. He spat on the ground near Clem's boot. "You leave those people to die back there, and you'll be running from me also." Rogers stood up straight, adjusting his rifle, while James fell him behind him.

Clem slowly panned down, laughing, looking at the wet spot on the pavement before looking up to shoot a sadistic grin at the bearded scout.

"Nobody cares about them. Right now it's about survival, and if they don't have the means, well, then we can't go sacrificing ourselves for them."

Rogers clenched his jaw and nudged a step forward. Clem let a hand drift from his hip to rest on the grip of a holstered sidearm. Turning to face Rogers, he squared his shoulders and stepped a half pace forward, inviting the threat. "Master Sergeant, I suggest you get your people un-fucked," he said without looking away.

The muscles in Jacob's neck tightened; his eyes locked on Clem's hand wrapped around the butt of the pistol. Instinctively, he pulled his own rifle closer. Distant combat echoed behind them, rattling through the trees, reminding them of the people dying at the camp.

Rogers shook his head slowly and his expression hardened before turning toward James, ignoring the others. "Let's go—lead us out. Jacob, keep that rifle up and ready; you kill anything that isn't us."

"What about them?" James asked, dipping his head at Clem as if he were an object rather than a person.

"Let them run if they like; it's not our job," Rogers said.

"You're all going to die. There aren't enough of you to make a difference," Clem shouted.

Jacob turned away to follow his leader; he met eyes with Masterson, who slightly dipped his chin before looking at Rogers. "Get to your people then meet us at Emmerson's Ridge. Do you know it?" Masterson said.

"I do," Rogers answered, stepping off into the destroyed convoy advancing in the direction of the camp.

***

They ran directly at the fighting, sacrificing caution for speed. Moving out of the narrow hills and onto an expanse of flat ground, James guided them to the shoulder of the paved road, Duke trotting by his side. The closer they got, the more Jacob could hear the sounds of screaming people, the noise fueling his adrenaline and blocking out the signals from his tired muscles begging him to quit.

At the cutoff where the paved surface of the road met the gravel, they spotted the first of them—a cloaked vehicle, its surface reflecting the same liquid sheen they'd seen in the valley. With no time to hide and without warning, a red turret materialized from atop the mirrored shell and rotated in their direction.

A bright flash burst out, and Jacob gasped for breath as a blue beam raced above his head, the oxygen in the air feeding whatever energy the projectile consumed. Jacob felt the heat on his neck, and the screech of the shot screamed at his ears.

He was bumped hard and knocked off course as Rogers moved him from the road and into the concealment of the trees. James's rifle barked somewhere ahead of them, single shots in rapid succession. "Contact left!" he shouted before firing another salvo.

Rogers stopped abruptly and dropped next to a tree, bringing up his own rifle. Jacob followed his movements, doing the same and dropping in line. Rogers's weapon joined the fight while Jacob spotted a target of his own—a broad-shouldered creature dressed in blue, the red stripes seeming to illuminate the sleeves of its arms. Covered by a wide glossy helmet, the creature's head swiveled. The helmet turned and a dark tinted screen locked in Jacob's direction.

The creature seemed to lean back slightly, surprised by his presence; its weapon rose to its shoulder and leveled out. Jacob was faster and already on target. He applied pressure to the trigger, feeling the buck of his rifle. The creature lurched back then spun, collapsing to the ground. James was back on his feet, running toward the camp as he shouted over Duke's barking for them to move up. Jacob could see the woods ahead flashing with the bright blue lights of the alien weapons, the report of the friendly rifles resistance fading.

Without consideration for their own safety, they rushed on, already committed and ready to put themselves in harm's way to shield the civilian withdrawal. Jacob exited the trees and dropped into the clearing of the athletic field. They had egressed at the center of the longest edge of the field. Rogers and James close to him, they were in a perfect flanking position.

Jacob could see the blockhouse far to his right, the structure now engulfed in blue flames. He searched a mass of friendlies just in front of the blockhouse, some fleeing while the wounded on the ground were making a final stand. He couldn't find Laura anywhere. The burning wreckage of the Blackhawk was on the opposite end of the field just inside a copse of trees—he prayed his family wasn't there. James moved close to him and grabbed his shoulder, taking his eyes from the burning wreckage of the helicopter and back to their immediate front.

"We'll look for them later … now, we fight," James said.

Jacob saw the creatures moving forward, firing at the wounded men on the ground. His anger blocked any recollection of fear. The aliens were close, less than fifty meters, and lined up in a makeshift skirmish line. Formed up like an opposing football team, this was a clean-up crew organized to finish those left in the fight. Marching ahead, they approached the blockhouse, weapons up and firing rapidly at anything to their front, the blue beams exploding and engulfing on contact, knocking the fleeing soldiers and civilians to the ground.

Watching the carnage, James snarled, “We have to stop this! This isn’t an attack … this is a massacre.”

Still in the aliens’ blind spot, the bearded man raised his rifle and snapped off three quick shots, took a deep breath, and fired again, laying down a base of fire into the blind profiles of the lined up creatures. The nearest alien crumpled; the others in the line, still preoccupied with the targets to their front, were oblivious to the attack on their flank. Jacob dropped to a knee and opened fire determinedly. Selecting targets of his own, he locked on center mass of each creature and watched them tumble with the impact of his rounds.

The remaining aliens turned, suddenly aware of the threat at their flank. At less than fifty meters away, they lunged, bringing their weapons up as they advanced. The Assassins were ready and already stable in their firing positions. Jacob was on his feet.

Stepping into the field, he stayed on the trigger, shoulder firing his M14 until the bolt of his rifle locked back. Jacob watched as his rounds cut through the creature's shirt, others smacking against its helmet and visor. Whatever armor the things wore, it was useless against Jacob's weapon.

The creatures were down, the gunfire ceased, and the Assassins found themselves alone now in the field, surrounded by the dead. James moved to one of the dead and kicked a heavy metallic rifle away from its gloved hand. He drew his knife and stood by the body encased in the blue suit. At over seven feet, the thing was taller than a human, its chest wide and shoulders at least double that of the largest man Jacob had ever seen.

"Looks like they skip leg day," James said, moving closer. He pointed at the creature's lower body, which appeared scrawny in comparison to the barrel chest.

"What are you doing?" Jacob asked.

Behind them, the fire around the downed chopper grew, the dry grass of the field and nearby woods now in flames. Rogers pointed in the direction of the helicopter. "We can't hang out here, the woods are going up," he shouted.

"I want to see what they look like," James said.

"What?"

"These things … I want to see their faces."

Rogers moved close and looked past them, posting himself at a standing watch. Unable to hold his own curiosity, he nodded the okay. "Hurry up then; get it done."

The bearded soldier probed and tugged at the corpse's armor. Duke paced back and forth restlessly, the scent of the beings still close in the air. Looking for a zipper or a way into the uniform, James rolled the thing over. He slunk back and looked down at his hands, now covered in bright red blood. "Well, they certainly bleed like us," he said.

"Well, they ain't us, so don't go getting attached," Rogers scorned, showing his impatience.

James found a locking fastener at the back of the creature's neck. With some struggle, he was able to break its grip. As he pulled down on the fastener, the fabric relaxed and loosened over the body. Soon it was so loose it draped off of the thing's shoulder blades, revealing a dull gray flesh covered in thick scales. When James went to touch the skin, the creature tried to rise, its back suddenly convulsing. Dropping down with force, James pressed a knee between the thing's shoulder blades and pinned it to the ground, listening to the alien wheeze its last breath.

He let off the pressure and rolled it to its back. The suit's grip released the helmet, allowing it to be easily lifted out of place from a locking collar and revealing a humanoid head. All the features of a human, its head was bald, the expressionless face showing evenly spaced eyes below perfect eyebrows, its lips thin and pressed tightly together.

"What the fuck? He looks just like us," Jacob gasped.

James pressed a finger into a hole just below the thing's collar bone. "Well, they weren't prepared for projectile weapons. If I had to take a guess, this blue suit works great against their ray guns."

"Energy weapons," Jacob added, reaching down to recover and examine the creature's rifle. It was simple in design from his engineer's vantage—a long cylinder that fit over the wearer's forearm and a lever mechanism fired the bolt. A series of red and blue lights shone brightly at the base, probably displaying the charge or weapon's strength. "It makes sense not to use projectiles—not having to replace a bullet—these things are probably rechargeable."

Looking down, Rogers shook his head. "So our body armor is useless against this blue shit. And their suits don't work against our rifles."

"Perfect matchup," James said sarcastically.

A low moan near the burning block house alerted them. Before Jacob could turn, Duke bounded through the field toward its source. His bark was different, more of a high pitched whine. He whimpered and stopped at a form near the building's porch, the dog's tail wagging frantically as he circled the figure. The men rushed ahead, finding a crumpled man struggling to stand. When he turned to face them, Jacob saw the bloodied bandage on the man's neck and the mournful face of Jesse Winslow.

Chapter 12

Wind blew through the trees, causing the upper branches to sway, the ends rattling as they touched. The light was fading, the sun's last rays casting orange slivers through naked trees. She could hear the cries echoing through the forest; other survivors, lost and alone, the same as her. She debated reaching out, searching for them; strength in numbers she thought. They ran through the forest, scattered and afraid. She listened to the rifle fire and the screams all around her. Looking at her pack filled with meager supplies and thinking about the way the others had enviously looked at her rifle, she thought otherwise. She did not know them, or if they could be trusted.

Laura lay hidden in the foliage of a dry creek bed, the vegetation too sparse to completely shelter her. A place where the ground dropped swiftly, the bank created an overhang that she was able to crawl into. A trail ran above her. If she held out, Jacob would return, and he would find them. Laura's heart still thudded away anxiously in her chest. She pulled the collar of her shirt up over her mouth to cover the sounds of heavy breathing, and to conceal the cloud of condensation that marked her position. Katy's face was buried in her hip; Laura could feel the warmth of her body pressed against her.

A curtain of roots hung down above her head. She heard the rustling and breaking of branches on the ground above—someone, or something, was stalking the trail. Laura's back was to the base of roughly packed dirt surface while tall grass and reeds surrounded the space directly to her front. She pushed the pack against the mound of earth so that it sheltered Katy from the wind channeling up the creek bed. As the noise above her grew louder, she cradled the rifle across her lap, allowing the end of the barrel to rest on her knees.

"Mama," Katy whispered.

Laura dropped a hand to the girl's head, cupping it, and brought her face down to meet her daughter's. "We have to be quiet now, okay?"

Trembling, Katy pursed her lips and pressed her face tighter to Laura's hip, her breathing barely audible. There was a crunching in the dry leaves above, then a whooshing through the air. A creature with long legs crashed into the dry creek bed to her front. The alien form landed hard, yet controlled, with its legs bending to absorb the impact. It darted a step forward then stopped. Its body was humanoid, but it movements were mechanical, not exactly like a machine but more like a freakishly muscled man. The thick-trunked creature twisted at the waist, its bulk shifting to look back behind it then back up at the elevated position it'd leapt from.

Laura held the rifle, biting down on the inside of her cheek and trying to suppress the urge to shake, scream, or call out. Her right hand squeezed the pistol grip of the M4 carbine, her thumb searching for the selector switch. A series of low beeps and clicks came from the creature's helmet. It turned its unarmed hand as if looking at a wrist watch then dipped its head, looking down and searching the depression where she hid. Its face mask focused on her, the thing's gaze traveling from Laura to Katy then back, its head tilting sideways like a curious dog.

She didn't wait, her thumb dropped the selector a single click and she pulled the trigger. The rifle bucked against her legs. She saw the puffs against the creature's chest, and the blue fabric tearing where rounds punched through its shirt. The thing dropped a step back. Laura imagined the look of surprise that must be on its face below the shielded helmet. Its right arm holding the weapon dropped and went slack; its left hand lay flat against its stomach then slowly slid up until it covered the already bleeding wounds. It staggered another half-step back before collapsing into the sand- and gravel-covered creek bed.

Laura tried to conceal her fear. She looked down and could see Katy shaking beside her, and the young girl's face contorted as she fought back tears. More footfalls landed heavily in the brush on the trail above her. She froze, looking down at the rifle still in her hands. She knew she couldn't fight them all; hiding would be the only way. Maybe if she dropped the weapon they would spare her. These weren't the same mindless monsters that came with the first meteor shower. The creature she just killed had hesitated as though it saw something that delayed it from killing her.

She had to try; she shoved the rifle into the thick leaves beside her and drug brush over their laps, lying back, hoping to hide. The ground shook as more of the creatures dropped in from above, crashing to the creek bed around the fallen alien. Laura opened her eyes, unable to resist the urge to look. She saw four of them; three the same as the one she killed, tall and broad-shouldered, but the fourth was smaller, more slender. The fourth wore gold stripes on its sleeves and moved in a smooth manner. Where the large beast lumbered, this one seemed to dance with graceful motions.

Laura couldn't take her eyes from the slender creature. She watched as the group examined its dead then turned to face her. The smaller figure stepped forward and stretched out a closed hand in her direction. Its golden-gloved fist opened slowly, revealing a thumb and six fingers; in its palm was a metallic disc. Laura watched as the disc blinked then flashed a blinding strobe. Instantly her body went numb. Paralyzed, she couldn't move. She attempted to fight it and desperately tried to reach for Katy to shield her, but her muscles wouldn't respond.

Her eyes shot straight ahead, unable to blink, unable to change focus. The slender alien turned to face the others, the clicks and beeps filling the air. The large creatures moved forward on stiff joints, lumbering toward her. One reached down, holding a golden bowl that he placed on the top of her head. Laura's muscles tensed at the same time her body flung into a spread eagle position. She felt distant, her mind a passenger in her body.

The clicks were gone, and then she heard a soft voice—not in her ears, but directly transmitted into her thoughts. "Keep the female with its cub. Deliver them to element six."

She struggled to turn to search for Katy. The slender creature approached her and knelt over her form. "There is no need to resist; you and your cub are safe now." The slender one put its hand to Laura's head and the world went dark.

Chapter 13

Crunched against debris at the side of the blockhouse, his shoulder and side speckled with burns, Jesse tried to push up to stand next to them. Gritting through the pain, he looked up at Jacob. "They're alive. She wasn't on the helicopter. She left with the others," he said.

"Which way did they go?"

Jesse clenched his eyes closed tight; Jacob could see that the man was fighting the pain. He opened them again and strained the muscles in his neck, attempting to get up. James removed a canteen from a carrier on his belt and opened it, allowing the wounded man to drink. Jesse gulped thirstily and paused. "We followed the trail, up toward the small cabins. I sent her north."

"Alone?" Jacob gasped.

Jesse dipped his chin and shook his head. "I'm sorry, Jacob. We tried to fight them back, but they outflanked us. They were on all sides. They got behind us; we pushed back this way but … those things went after them. They fought through us and went after the civilians."

Movement in the brush behind them revealed two men creeping out of the woods and into the clearing. A soldier dressed in a soiled uniform, a young man in civilian clothes beside him. The soldier carried a rifle loosely in his arms. The other man had burns to his face and neck. The armed man spotted them and rushed in their direction, dragging the wounded man with him. As they approached them, the wounded man collapsed to the ground, exhausted. The soldier squatted by his side. He looked up at Jacob, and the others then searched the surrounding field.

"Where's Masterson?" the soldier gasped between labored breaths. "Where the hell is Clem?"

James shook his head, taking the canteen from Jesse and passing it to the new arrivals. "He's not coming. Can you tell me what happened here?"

"Fuck," the soldier gasped, dropping to the ground on both knees. "He's not coming? What do you mean he's not com—?"

Jacob edged toward him, interrupting. "Where are the civilians, the other survivors?"

The wounded man pulled himself together and sat up. He put his hands on his face and rubbed away dirt and grime from his forehead. He looked at Jacob intently. "I know you; you're the one with the little girl."

"Yes," Jacob said eagerly. "Where are they?"

The man looked down at the ground then met Jacob's stare. "I'm sorry. Those things—just so fast, they—they took them." The man closed his eyes tight and looked away.

"Where are they? I have to know."

The man swallowed hard and pointed in the direction of the cottages. "I barely got away myself."

Jacob got to his feet and faced the trail. Stepping off, he moved out alone. James and Rogers were quickly up and following him. Rogers turned back and pointed to Jesse struggling to his feet. "Salvage what you can from here then take this one and get to the bunker at the end of the trail—"

"By the radio tower," the soldier answered.

"That's the place. Now go."

Jacob moved on, walking the center of the trail. He noticed the others following him and looked back. "You don't have to do this; I understand the odds," he said, his voice breaking.

James increased his pace. Not answering, he moved past Jacob, taking the point position and moving down the trail filled with nightmarish scenes. "We'll find them," he said, ignoring the obvious all around him.

Bodies were strewn along the trail, many of them scorched by the blue flames; open wounds cauterized by the heat of the plasma weapons. Smoke was billowing through the woods, mixed with the smell of burning plastics and building materials. Fires raged all around them. Ahead, Jacob could see the one-room cottages fully engulfed, the orange flames lighting the forest floor. He moved past them, feeling the heat of the fires, stepping over the bodies of fallen soldiers and civilians, checking each as he passed.

He stopped and looked down at the ground. The packed dirt of the trail was broken and disturbed. He knelt and fumbled with the loose soil. Duke was at his side, whimpering and sniffing at the ground.

James pointed off the trail. "The branches are broken, the grass bent against the others … they left the trail here," he said. James swiveled his head, giving a worried glance back at the flames. "We'll need to hurry."

The bearded scout broke the trail, stepping into the pucker brush, his hand pointing to the signs of a cut trail. He nearly stumbled over the body of a young man in civilian clothes, the back of the man burnt down to his exposed ribcage. James stepped to the side and pointed; without saying, the others knew they were on the right path. Coming out of the thick cover, Duke ran ahead and sat on another trail, this one far narrower and led along a dry creek bed. The dog moved ahead, leading the way with the others close behind.

The forest was suddenly quiet, only the roaring of the fire and the crackling of burning trees making any sounds. The light had faded; if not for the eerie back glow of the burning forest, it would have been too dark to see each other. James put down a palm, slowing the others and bringing them in close before pointing down at sets of odd boot prints on the trail. Large and oval shaped, they pressed deeply into the soil and looked to be composed of hundreds of tiny spikes. James stepped off, leading them on before pausing again.

Duke was ahead on the trail, pacing anxiously and whining as he moved on and off the trail to show the way. James cautiously followed along beside the animal and made his way to a steep drop-off. He weaved left and navigated his way off the trail with the others close behind. James stopped in a gravel depression and touched his gloved hand to the soil. When he raised it, it was covered with sticky blood. He then waved his hand along the sand and gravel bed, covered with more of the odd boot prints nearly lost on the loose soil. "A group of them stopped here; one didn't leave vertical," he said, sticking a gloved finger into a puddle of blood.

Jacob followed him into the creek bed, the despair building in his body, fearing what he may find. He spun, looking at the boot prints and the blood on the sand. A lingering fear began building in his stomach. He stopped and was caught by a sudden flash of color, bright nylon fabric against the bank. He rushed ahead and found Laura's backpack, her rifle and a spent shell casing on the ground beside it. Jacob took a step forward and dropped to his knees, pulling the backpack to his chest.

"Jacob, over here," Rogers called, following Duke over a rise on the far side of the creek.

A bare foot exposed from the surrounding grass. Jacob moved closer, climbing the rise and finding a scene of burnt and discarded bodies scattered among the small clearing. "My God, they killed them … all of them," he gasped.

Rogers shook his head in disagreement as he bent over and lifted a stuffed bear. "No, only the men," he said, indicating the bodies. "Check them for yourself. All the women and children are gone, and all their belongings are left where they were dropped. They were taken, Jacob."

Chapter 14

The television was too loud. Tin echoes recalling the previous day's news, traffic, and highlights of the weather. She had fallen asleep in front of the TV. Jacob would be home soon, she should get up. She squinted. Bright sunlight from an open window; she forgot to close the blinds last night. Somewhere in her subconscious she smelled wood smoke, distant but alarming. A tiny voice in the back of her mind began to scream *something is wrong*, pulling her into the present.

"Mommy."

Laura rubbed her face and jerked her head to the side. Prying open tired eyes, she looked into an unfamiliar space. Shocked awake, her now conscious brain struggled to move into this new place. She was not home. She was lying on an overstuffed sofa, covered with an afghan blanket. The room was a cliché 1960s theme—pastel walls, shag carpet, a wood-paneled console television along a wall, playing a black-and-white image with a looped broadcast. There were family photos on the wall, filled with people that she didn't recognize.

"Mommy," Katy said, shaking her arm.

Laura pulled her in, suddenly remembering her last thoughts when she was hiding in the woods, trying to keep Katy safe. But now Katy was here and she was clean, wearing a yellow cotton gown. Her hair was soft, washed and tied back, a concave bowl attached to the top of her head. Remembering, Laura's hand swung up, checking her own head; she wore the same device. She noticed she was also dressed in the same yellow clothing.
"Katy … where—?"

"You were sleeping, Momma. The people gave us food," she said.

Laura pushed herself up, feeling disoriented and struggling to recall the gaps in her memory. In the corner of the room was a small dining table; on the top was a brown tray with cut sandwiches and stainless steel cups. "Did you eat it?" she said, tension building in her voice. "Who put it there?"

A hissing sound, the clunk of a lock, and the door swung in. A backlit figure stood in the opening and lurched a cautious step forward. "The consumables are safe; we have no reason to poison you."

The voice was soft and familiar; it appeared in her thoughts rather than her ears. Katy was on her feet before Laura could stop her. She moved past the being and climbed to the table, grabbing a sandwich. She took a bite and looked back at her mother, smiling.

Dressed head to toe in baby-blue linens that reminded Laura of hospital smocks, the creature slid another step toward her, and the heavy door swung closed behind it. Feminine features, tanned skin, petite and slender, it was smaller than any woman Laura had ever met. The thing's head was free of hair, its face perfectly shaped like a store mannequin. Its lips moved when it spoke in a foreign tongue, but Laura was somehow able to comprehend the words. "Are you comfortable?"

With graceful movements, the creature moved closer. It looked at Laura and blinked its piercing blue eyes. Passing through the room, it sat gently on a chair across from her and smiled with perfect rose-tinted lips.

Laura looked away, repulsed; her head spinning.

"Don't be alarmed; it's your knowledge plate. The discomfort will soon pass as your system adjusts," the alien said.

Laura's eyes focused on Katy at the table. Again she went to speak, but the creature stopped her with an uplifted six-fingered hand. Laura's gaze found the table where a notepad and pen lay just in front of her.

"The food is safe. It meets all of your nutritional needs," the alien said.

"Why am I here? What do you want with us?" Laura sat up. Leaning forward, she let her hand pass over the notepad and palmed the pen. She pulled it into her grip and slipped her hand to her thigh.

"Why are *you* here?" the thing responded in turn.

"I don't understand; you brought me here."

"Then you concede that we were here first?" The thing nodded and crossed its hands into its lap. "Understanding will be the key to our partnership."

Laura shifted in position. Sitting up further, she looked the alien in the eye, squeezing the pen in her grip, emboldened by the firmness of it. "Partnership? Who are you?"

"I am Thera, your guide."

"What do you want?"

"I am but one of many. I don't want anything."

Laura, not waiting any longer, lunged at the creature, arms outstretched, stabbing down with the tip of the pen. It did no good. Before she cleared half the distance, the alien shifted to the side smoothly and opened its hand, freezing her. She fell back into the cushions. Her legs still bent, she tilted to the side awkwardly, her eyes now fixed on the ceiling.

"Your knowledge plate gives away your intentions. You have shown strong restraint characteristics, Mrs. Laura Anderson; your peers were not so cordial in our first meeting." The alien paced across the room to the exit and turned the knob. The creature looked back to Laura and flashed six fingers. Laura felt immediate relief, the feeling returning to her muscles, her heart rapidly beating in her chest.

"When you have rested, we will have more to discuss."

Laura's head panned to Katy, who was still sitting at the table, unaware of the tension in the room. The door opened and two men entered, both dressed in dark-blue coveralls. The taller of the two carried a clipboard and a bundle of folded, yellow clothing. The shorter man stepped forward, smiling. He wore a close-cropped beard, the rest of his head nearly bald. She noticed that both men were wearing the gold discs on their heads. The tall man waved to Katy as he passed the alien that was leaving the room, the door closing behind it.

"Mrs. Anderson?" the short man said in a thick French accent. "It is good to see you awake. Are you finding everything you need?"

Laura stretched her back, numbness fading as blood rushed to her muscles. Her hand moved up to squeeze the pained muscles in her neck. She pushed forward and quickly got to her feet, edging away from the visitors and standing between them and Katy. "Who are you?"

The shorter man smiled and dropped his hands, showing palms in a submissive stance. "My name is Francis; this is Ernesto. We're friends; you have nothing to fear from us."

"Am I … am I a prisoner?" Laura asked, her head spinning in confusion.

The men laughed patronizingly. "No, of course not; no more than we are. You've been rescued." The man focused on Laura's shocked expression. "Does this look like a prison? You're safe now."

Laura stepped back and allowed herself time to survey the space. She noticed a covered window on the far wall. The short man caught her gaze and followed it. He waved a hand toward the thick drapes. "Yes, it's okay," he said. "Please, have a look."

Laura backed away then slowly stepped to the wall, casting a wide berth around the two strangers. She put her fingertips to the heavy drapes and pulled back the fabric.

Bright sunlight bled into the room as she peeled back the curtain. Laura moved and pressed against the glass. She was in a house at the end of a cul-de-sac. In front was a lawn of thick uncut grass and a car in the driveway on flat tires. Along the blacktop surface sat a row of cookie-cutter homes, garbage stacked along the curbs. Beyond them, she could see a tall fence. It didn't look natural, its material smooth and out of place; not metallic, but not wood or stone either. "We have some work to do, but this community will do nicely. We have full support from the Creators."

Pressing close, in the distance she could see people walking the tree-lined street—all women and children. More of the figures in gold sleeves wandered among them, all being watched over by the large, more stout creatures. She was in a community, but she didn't recognize any of it. She looked back at the men. "What is this place?"

"It's a start."

Chapter 15

Jacob, Rogers, and James now lay shivering in damp grass, a dense fog rolling into the valley out of the surrounding hills. Fire glowed in the distance, the woods fully engulfed and no teams of fire fighters to battle them. Through the warm tones of the fire, Jacob could see the glistening frost on the grass. He wished he'd taken the time to wear warmer gear, the dirt and blood-covered blouse and armor doing little against the chilled morning air. His food was gone, and only a tiny bit of water sloshed around in a near-empty canteen.

Their packs had been left back in the thick of the woods. All they carried now were their rifles and ammunition. They'd spent the night in the foundation of a burned-out gas station, cautiously moving to their current spot long before dawn. This bit of real estate was on the approach to a small village. They'd seen lights there from the high ground and, from markings on the trails and vehicle traffic, believed that's where the captives were taken.

James was on watch, and Jacob knew he should sleep, but between the shivering, ache in his belly, and the restless thoughts, he found it impossible. He lifted his head and looked to the western horizon; there was still no sun. He forced a roll and felt the dog move anxiously behind his calves. No pause in the big man's heavy breathing beneath his poncho liner, Rogers ignored his movements.

Cautiously working to his side, he pulled up the binoculars from the grass to his front and surveyed the terrain. James positioned them on the slope of a ridge distant to the village. They lined up so that a far off streetlight was directly ahead, like a beacon, guessing at what the terrain would bring in the daylight. With the coming of dawn, Jacob could just barely make out the manmade shapes of walls and peaked roofs. A lone street lamp illuminated an iron gate maybe a half mile from their hide.

Suspiciously, there were neither people nor the Deltas—or more deadly Red Sleeves—in sight. Several vehicles had moved down the road in both directions, both entering and exiting the gate. Jacob wanted to get closer, attempt to enter the gate or climb the wall, but Rogers wouldn't allow it. The plan was to lie in overwatch and develop a strategy. They were on their own, and no help would come if they were compromised.

James edged closer and looked over the same space. "If they have sentries out, they must be behind the walls."

"Can this be done?"

James furrowed his brow as he focused on the far off gate. "I guess that depends on what we plan to do."

"If you all aren't talking about coffee then shut the hell up," Rogers mumbled, moving under the poncho liner. He pulled back the blanket and tussled to his side before propping up on his elbows.

The sun was slowly breaking the horizon. Jacob watched as the black shapes became a large, gated community. A tall fence moved out to the left and right. A well maintained blacktop road met the gate. He was punched on the shoulder and caught Rogers handing him a small hunk of jerky. Jacob grabbed it and stuffed it in his cheek before putting his eyes back on the binoculars. "When do we go down?" Jacob whispered.

"Pssst," James hissed. "We got movement."

Jacob saw a vehicle convoy approaching the gate; the tickle in his ear let him know it was their vehicles. Four personnel carriers in a straight line, they slowed and stopped just short of the gate. A red-sleeved beast exited the first carrier and bound to the gate, pushing it back, allowing the convoy to enter, and closing it behind the last vehicle.

"Strange … they opened the gate themselves, no guard posted," Rogers whispered.

Within minutes the tickle was gone, and they were again alone in the high grass.

James sighed and backed away, catching Jacob's stare. "What?" he asked.

"I'm sorry, Jacob, but this isn't going to work," James whispered.

"Now hold—"

Rogers tilted his wrist, looking down. "He's right, best case we get everyone killed. They're running some sort of base out of there. We can't take it alone."

Jacob turned to Rogers. "Like you said … no guard."

Rogers grimaced. "That just means they are confident."

"Or they have an inner perimeter," James added.

"If we're not here to get them out, why the hell *are we* here?" Jacob said.

"Recon, maybe take a head."

"A head?"

"Sure every enemy has a leader; maybe we can kill or capture one. James, see if you can sneak around that wall; travel east and look for a secondary entrance. I'll take Jacob to the west. Don't engage; we need to see what's in there."

James nodded, pulling his gear in and stuffing it into pockets on his vest. "Back here in four hours then?"

"Wait no longer than that. If we aren't here, fall back to the bunker." Rogers rolled to the right and sat up. He folded the poncho liner then opened a small pack and removed four grenades still in the tubes, handing two to James before placing the other two in pouches on his chest rig. He stuffed the blanket into the small pack and readied his rifle. "Go ahead, James, I'll give you a five-minute start before we move. If you hear shooting, don't try to back us up, just bee-line to the bunker."

James grinned. "Understood, but I can't make any promises."

Before Rogers could argue, James was on his feet moving down the hill with the dog close by his side. Jacob watched the man glide down the hill and disappear into heavy vegetation at the base. Soon there was no sign that he'd ever been there. Rogers looked at Jacob. "You ready?"

He nodded and signaled a thumbs up. Jacob stood and fell in line behind Rogers. They moved away from the gate, staying just below the hilltop, careful not to profile themselves against the rising sun. Jacob felt good to be back on his feet, the movement helping to warm his cold and cramped muscles. They passed down a draw and toward a thick batch of vegetation. Rogers set the pace, cutting back and forth over easier-to-travel terrain. They moved around a low, open area, sticking to the shadows of the hill.

Jacob looked back at the high ridge behind him, its high grass now swallowed in shadows. Looking further east, he could see a sloping face that overlooked the west wall. Rogers pointed to it and dropped to his knees then slowly leopard-crawled into a batch of low grass.

Jacob could tell by the growth patterns of the vegetation that this is where the field would have been cut to before the attacks. The grass went from a tall, brushed clean appearance to more wild and mixed with weeds and scrub brush. Looking closer at the high walls as the sun hit the surface, Jacob suddenly could see that it was different. "Rogers, that material, what is it?"

Holding the binoculars, Rogers scanned the fence. “A type of carbon fiber maybe? This has to be a base, why else build a wall?”

Rogers pointed to a batch of playground equipment surrounded by a small walking path that led into an open slot on the wall filled with a narrow gate. Jacob put his rifle to his cheek and scanned the low ground ahead. No movement, the area appeared completely unoccupied. The pedestrian gate hung closed and a broken sapling slapped against the surface of the nearby wall.

On the far side of the walls, shingled rooftops glistened in the morning sun and the shadow of the hills behind them receded. Clouds of smoke in the distance drifted lazily on the horizon. Using the binoculars, they spotted a road that meandered through the small community. Rogers tapped Jacob’s shoulder then indicated an elevated mound near the edge of the clean grass. It was higher than the rest of the nearly flat ground that ringed the fence, but they would have to cross open terrain to reach it.

Jacob nodded a reply and followed his leader toward the position. Wading through high grass, Jacob could feel the pace pick up. He felt the urgency; they needed to get set before the sun completely broke the high ground behind them and washed them in daylight. As the shadows pulled toward them, Jacob instinctively swallowed at a tickle at the back of his neck. His muscles tightened. “Rogers,” he whispered above the labored breath of his movement.

“I feel it too, just keep moving.”

Rogers scrambled ahead and dove into high grass as the vibration intensified. Jacob low-crawled, following Rogers’s boots up the incline of the mound. He could hear the sound of the vehicles, the *whooshing* their engines made defying gravity as they forced away from the ground.

He crawled up until the ground leveled out then they turned and pushed their weapons in front of them, faces down in the earth, taking labored breaths from both exhaustion and adrenaline. When he dared, he slowly lifted his head just high enough so that he could peek through the tall grass. They’d closed the distance to the pedestrian gate to less than a football field.

It was in easy firing range now. The sapling no longer swung with the breeze. Beside it stood a tall, red-sleeved soldier. The creature carried a weapon at the low ready while a larger group of them were forming up inside the wall with the vehicles inside the now open gate.

“You think they know we’re here?” Jacob whispered. “What made them rush out like that?”

“No, if they knew, we’d be dead, just stay cool.”

Jacob’s eyes met Rogers’s stare. “Okay, what do we do now?”

The hardened soldier pressed closer to the earth and dipped his chin. Jacob’s eyes followed the motion and saw them—a large group of people, mostly women and children, walking two by two in a long column on the path. They were flanked on both sides by the red-sleeved aliens. As they got closer, Jacob could see they were being followed by Deltas. Moving differently now, they marched in straight lines, their black eyes locked straight ahead.

Jacob began to speak, but Rogers silenced him with a finger to his lips. The civilians carried no belongings. Women gripped the hands of children; those too young to walk were carried. The Deltas seemed to focus on moving the civilians forward, while the Red Sleeves were on lookout, searching for threats. As the group neared the gate, more Reds exited, these also joined by the smaller, gold-sleeved creatures.

The approaching civilians stopped short of the gate. They were quickly grouped together and formed into a long line with the Deltas directly behind them and to the side, effectively fencing them off. One by one, a Gold Sleeve would leave the gate and approach a family unit. Dividing a parent and children from the others, the alien would then escort these small groups through the gates, a new gold member replacing it before identifying a new batch of civilians.

On more than one occasion, a civilian would hesitate or resist instructions to follow; these would somehow be dropped to the ground then carried by a Red. Soon the entire group of civilians was inside the walls. The Deltas turned and began moving back down the path into the direction they'd come from with the Red Sleeves forming up to follow them.

The pedestrian gate was now closed; the Reds inside the wall vanished.

"What just happened?" Jacob whispered, seeing the last of the marching Deltas fade from sight.

"They're herding us; using the Deltas as sheep dogs, and those damn Reds as shepherds. That explains what we found. They killed off all the men, gathered the women and children, and took them here."

"Why?"

"I don't know, but I think they're safe. Why take them and go to all of this trouble just to kill them?"

"Why do *any* of this? What are we going to do?"

Before Rogers could answer, the snapping of distant gunfire echoed through the valley, a single gunshot quickly followed by two more.

Rogers grunted and pushed away. "And that would be James. It's time to move."

Chapter 16

Clem rolled his shoulders, forcing aches and cramps from his weary muscles. His pack and rifle lay at his feet. So far he'd managed to keep up with the younger men, but at over sixty years old, he knew his days were catching up with him. It took them all night to make the climb to the top of Emmerson's Ridge, and now they were all paying for it. Exhausted and pushed to the limits, the stress of moving through the enemy territory had worn heavily on him. Looking around, for the first time, Clem began to regret having joined up with this group.

He was doing fine on his own. Surviving the initial attacks then living quietly in a secluded cabin between the American lines to the west and the Canadian forces behind him to the east. He'd managed to stay hidden from the waves of refugees, and even score a way to trade goods with the passing patrols. The American soldiers were always willing to give up a few rounds of ammunition or a ration pack for a portion of his homemade wine and spirits. Masterson and his instructors had become some of his best customers—probably why he allowed them near his place after the big bomb dropped and then allowed himself to be convinced to go with them.

The old man lowered himself to the ground and leaned back against his pack. He was no stranger to this life. Not so much a soldier, but having spent a career working with the intelligence service, Clem had paid his dues on the ground and in the bush. Still, he was no infantry commander, and he felt at odds in his current situation. Surrounded by the grunts and their leaders, he felt exposed and vulnerable. His trade had called for being alone or in a small group, hidden in plain sight. Clem knew he didn't belong; he was used to working with a scalpel, whereas the tool of choice for these men was a chainsaw.

There were caches of food and ammunition hidden along the ridge and Masterson had his men moving up and down it, securing the goods. Men stacked bundles of stockpiled weapons and ammunition, all makes and model of military arms hidden there weeks ago.

Clem watched as the veteran soldier approached him. He waved a hand, inviting the tired soldier to sit. Masterson nodded in recognition of the gesture and turned to look back down the valley before slowly lowering himself to a knee. The man was breathing hard and sweat lined his brow. Clem extended a hand and tossed the man a canteen filled with cold water. The soldier put it to his lips and drank thirstily.

Masterson dropped to the ground and let the canteen fall by his side. "You know, I thought we were winning again; maybe had the black-eyed bastards pushed back. After everything we went through, the numbers we've lost, I thought we were finally gaining ground again.

"But this—whatever this is—Clem, you know in the last forty-eight hours we've lost everything we've gained? I don't know what we have left to fight for. For the first time, I don't know what in the hell to do or how in the hell to do it."

Clem nodded, looking along the cluster of men hidden in the rocks and stumps along the ridgeline, most of them now asleep under ponchos while a small working party was reloading magazines and sorting through supplies. He reached across the ground and retrieved the canteen, returning it to his belt. He sighed and leaned farther into his pack. "You need to cut them loose," Clem said.

"Loose?!" Masterson said, unable to hide the surprise in his voice.

The old man dipped his chin and used a hand to rub his wrinkled brow. "You had what? Two hundred men three days ago; a hundred yesterday and now down to forty, maybe fifty, still able to fight.

You need to create a smaller footprint, and you need to do it fast before they are all gone. Send them to ground."

"Not much of a plan."

"It's the best I got for you, Matt," Clem said, using the old soldier's nickname. "Divide them up, pick a leader, give them instructions to go out and raise hell for the enemy. Or send them east to see if the lines are still holding there. Hell, just tell them to hide and wait it out; better than losing the lot of them on some empty country road.

"This isn't giving up; it's what defending armies do when confronted by a greater force. We can't face this head on. They have the weapons and they have the numbers. It's time for the Republican Guard to fade back into the population, preserve their numbers, and prepare for the resistance."

Not missing the reference to the invasion of Iraq, Masterson looked back at Clem. "I know you said you were some sort of cop at one time, but really, who the hell are you?"

"I'm just a tired old man with too many scars."

Masterson looked Clem in the eye, frustration showing on his face. "That's it then? I tell them to hide and wait it out?"

Clem shook off the comment and reached into a side pocket of his oilskin jacket. He pulled out a stainless steel flask and removed the cap, putting the neck to his nose before taking a long sip. He pursed his lips and grinned before passing the flask to Masterson.

"You know, I've been thinking about this since day one. The meteorites, the Day of the Darkness; that was just to soften us up, make us weak and destroy our defenses, get us to tighten up behind walls. Hell … and that's exactly what we did, just like they expected us to. We consolidated our forces, our people."

Masterson took a sip and held back a burning cough. He nodded. "That's what we did at Meaford and similar places across the globe, barricaded behind walls."

Clem pointed at him. "And you know what else? Look at the way we abandoned our conventional weapons, tanks, and fighter aircraft when we lost the airfields and oil reserves. That's all gone now with the waves of those Deltas. We settled in for a long war with them, and now look.

"Then came the first of those damn balloons soaring overhead, positioning themselves like landing craft in the English Channel. The way they hit the ground with the bombs, destroying population centers and bases, once again softening us up before landing their troops. And look at them now, the lack of aircraft, not a single drone. Why is that?"

Masterson shrugged as he drank again this time more heavily, straining to keep up with the old man's thoughts. He held in the liquid and shrugged before passing back the flask.

"Because they don't have any, that's why. I think they're stuck here. These aren't Viking raiders, these are Roman conquerors; hell, pilgrims even, and we're the Indians this time. I don't think they're much different from us, maybe some new gadgets and tricks to kill us, but I'd imagine their tech is nothing outrageous; if it was, we'd already be dead.

"Those were drop ships, and—I believe—on a one-way trip at that. Those things aren't here to steal shit from our planet and leave. Nope, that'd be too simple. They're here for the planet. They're here to colonize. They want it all, and best I figure, they aren't leaving."

Masterson laughed. "And what do you plan to do about it?"

"I sure as hell won't surrender, and we're dead if we all stay bunched up like this. Maybe in small teams we've got a chance." Clem chuckled. "I've been watching their movements, and they've all come from and returned to the same direction. I think one of those drop ships landed close to here and set up a base. I’m going to see if I can find it.”

“And if you do?”

Clem smiled. “Well, hopefully kill a bunch of them and live long enough to brag about it over a jar of homemade shine,” he said, taking another long sip and passing the flask back. “How about you, Matt? You think you got another war left in you?”

The old soldier grinned. “You know, Clem, I’ve been fighting on the other side my entire life; guess it’s time to see how the gorillas do it.”

Chapter 17

Laura tried to remain calm; she put on a strong face for Katy, who was completely unaware of their situation and enjoying the new surroundings. The home was warm and clean, she found the kitchen lightly stocked with food, the refrigerator held a metallic pitcher of water, and there was even bread on the counter. All the drawers and cupboards were empty of china or glass, supplied instead with a set of plastic plates and cups.

Laura searched the old house, finding closets cleaned out, dresser drawers empty. Moving from room to room, every window was sealed shut, and every door locked from the outside. She entered the small bathroom and tried the faucets, finding the water hot. *"How can this be? What is this place?"*

A knock at the front door, followed by the clunk of the lock, frightened her. She rushed from the bathroom and took a position between Katy and the entrance. The door slowly opened, revealing the smiling face of the short Frenchman. "Sorry to alarm you, Mrs. Anderson, it is time for reception."

Laura backed away, lifting an arm to shield Katy behind her. "Francis, I don't understand why you are doing this. Just let us go."

The man looked at her with a shocked expression. "Go? Why would you wish to leave? Where would you go, the camps? Would you prefer that over a warm home and the food you have been provided? Is that what you would prefer for your child?"

"I had that before—"

"And you have it now. Please, Mrs. Anderson, it would be unwise to decline reception. It is required, and not attending will have consequences."

Laura backed away, getting closer to Katy.

"They would take her from you," the man said, looking to Katy. "Please, just do as they ask. You'll see; it gets easier."

"How do you know, Francis? Why do you trust them?"

"What's not to trust? They feed us, they provide us shelter, and they protect us from the martyrs."

"The martyrs?"

"Those who preceded the Messenger."

"You mean the Deltas?"

"Yes, of course."

"But they made them," Laura said. "They created those monsters!"

"They made everything; they are the Creators. Please, we cannot be late," the man pleaded.

Laura ignored him. "Why did they attack us?"

The man turned and looked at the open door. Laura could see people moving past it, all dressed in the dark-blue and the soft-yellow gowns. "You mustn't speak this way; you shouldn't even think it. Blasphemy is not tolerated among them. Please, just come; all will be explained."

Laura could tell by his words that the man was worried; not only for her, but for himself as well. She turned and held Katy's hand before looking back at him. He smiled eagerly and waved a hand, ushering them ahead of him. She took a deep breath and told herself to relax, this wasn't submission, she was just learning about them; she would find what she needed to know and look for a way out.

“Okay,” she said softly and stepped through the doorway and onto a narrow sidewalk.

The roadway in front of the small house was now filled with a parade of people. The helmeted Reds lined the sidewalk like security guards, searching the group for threats. Francis moved close to her. “Now just walk with me. Do not talk to anyone; communication with other new arrivals is frowned upon.

“If you have a question or need assistance, ask me and no one else. Do you understand?”

Laura nodded her acknowledgement without looking at him. She was now in the mix, Katy walking close beside her. The road was filled with clusters of women and walking children, each with a man in dark-blue gowns of their own. She looked ahead at the end of the road between the houses and could just barely make out their destination.

“Where are the men?” Laura asked.

“There are no men, except for those like myself.”

“And what are you?”

“Think of me as your sponsor, to assist with your transition.”

Laura looked down at Katy. "Are you okay, hun?"

Francis grinned. "She is fine. Children are more receptive to the knowledge plate; her level of understanding already exceeds ours. Her mind is more open and less resistant to the transition."

Laura hesitated, a chill moving down her spine, causing her legs to stiffen. Ahead was the globe, the mammoth pumpkin-shaped orb now buried into the flat ground with only its top remaining exposed. Missing portions of it showed entry hatches and openings. She saw Deltas along the outside of it moving earth and cutting away vegetation, making room for vehicles and formations of gathering Reds. At the front was a large stage. The procession of people was leaving the road and approaching it.

"Francis," she said with fear in her voice.

He gripped her free hand and squeezed it. "What you are feeling is normal. I was afraid at my first reception as well. Soon you will understand."

A formation of Reds moved them tighter together until they were all clustered at the front of the ship. Unlike other crowds of this size, the group was silent, only the breathing and rustling of their clothing providing any ambient noise. Above the large platform, an entryway appeared at the side of the orb. A group of Reds exited and lined the edges of the platform, soon followed by a group of the smaller creatures with gold sleeves. Like the guide, Thera, these wore no helmets. They formed a straight line along the face of the platform then knelt low. Behind them, a blue light shone in the entrance and out walked a male dressed head to toe in glimmering gold. It was taller than the golden-sleeved guides, but nowhere near the size of the Reds. The crowd let out a combined gasp as the thing moved forward, stopping directly in line of the gold-sleeved guides.

She felt Francis squeeze on her hand. She knew it was his reminder to remain calm. Francis put his lips close to her ear. "This is the Messenger," he whispered.

The thing moved to the center of the line then raised its arms. Laura looked and watched as the crowd around her knelt, taking the same position as the guides on the platform. A pressure from the top of her head urged her down. She dropped to her knees, holding her eyes closed against the pressure. The creature waited until everyone had followed suit. Laura heard an angered shout near the front and looked up; an older woman stood defiantly shouting, her hand pointed at the Messenger. He flipped a wrist in her direction. She crumpled to the ground and was quickly collected by Reds that moved in from the perimeter. The woman was hurriedly shuttled out of sight.

She returned the squeeze and looked down at Katy, giving the girl a small smile. Katy looked up playfully and leaned into her mother, the young girl somehow sensing the seriousness of the gathering.

The Messenger lowered his arms, and the Golds rose back to their feet, the crowd rising with them.

Stepping to the edge of the platform, the Messenger began to speak. Once again the words came to Laura as thoughts, not transmissions through her ears. "We have come home to you, and now you are saved. You are now a part of us, as you have always been. This we accept. You will be provided for; all of your needs will be met. We welcome you into our civilization; any rejection of this will not be tolerated."

The Messenger stepped back and looked to his right, then nodded. A pair of red-sleeved guards emerged, holding the older women who'd shouted the outburst earlier. They brought her forward. The woman's body appeared paralyzed, frozen into an already kneeling position.

A pair of guides emerged out of the blue light, pushing a large golden cauldron. The Messenger approached the old woman and removed the knowledge plate from the crown of her skull. Freed from its hold, the woman began to struggle, yet unable to break the grip of the Reds holding her tight. The Messenger waved them forward. They stopped just short of the cauldron, shaking the woman and forcing her to her feet. The Messenger gripped the back of the woman's head and looked back into the crowd.

"Those who refuse our message will be martyred." The Messenger forced the woman's head into the cauldron. Her body convulsed, fighting against the grip of the guards. The old woman fought, legs kicking, splashing the black oily liquid from the pot. Suddenly, her body relaxed and the Messenger released his grip on her head. The guards pulled the old woman back. She stood upright and opened eyes as black as coal. The crowd let out a collective gasp.

Katy buried her head into her mother's waist. The Messenger stood with his arms raised; Laura looked back to the front, the pressure in her knowledge plate forcing her eyes to remain open. Silenced, with all of their eyes to the front, the crowd stood fixed on the woman's transformed body.

Raising his hands, the Messenger began to speak when its head snapped back as a gunshot cracked through the air. Laura felt the release of the knowledge plate when the Messenger's head slumped forward, its forehead destroyed as two more holes thumped into its chest. Gunshots echoed in the midst of Reds rushing forward to surround the Messenger.

Screaming, the crowd panicked while Laura stood still, a smile forming on her face.

"The Assassins reject your message," she said.

Chapter 18

"Holy shit!" Jacob shouted, running for the tree line. "Whatever just happened, they are *pissed*." The air was erupting with the vibration of the alien vehicles coming to life. Blue bolts of light ripped across the far horizon.

"Get up the ridge and into the tree line," Rogers yelled.

Jacob led the way, stumbling through the high grass, colliding with the steep slope of the ridge at a full sprint. He twisted his gloved hands into the thick vegetation and pulled himself up, his legs pumping for traction. The *voomp* of the enemy gunfire growing louder and nearer to them, Jacob summited the steep hill and reached back, pulling Rogers up behind him. They low-crawled into the cover of high trees overlooking the walled community.

"There," Rogers said, pointing.

Cutting across the low ground and running close to the fence, they spotted James, the dog close by his side. Splashes of blue raced by him, the shots going up and smacking into the sides of the far off hills. Rogers raised his rifle, spotting the first of James's pursuers—a Red in close pursuit.

"We're in it now," Rogers said, pulling the trigger. Firing several rounds, the Red tumbled to the ground. James lifted his head. Spotting them on the high ridgeline, he corrected his course and ran directly to them.

In his peripheral vision, Jacob saw the pedestrian gate open and three Reds move into the open. Unaware of them on the ridge, the Reds turned to the west, attempting to cut James off. He turned and squared his chest to them. Putting the rifle to his cheek, he eased off the safety and took aim at the tail runner. He let loose a salvo of five rounds that left the three Reds dead on the ground. A blue splash of plasma smacked the trees over his head, raining down flaming debris. Jacob spun back to the front; the number of James's pursuers had doubled, and then tripled.

Many were firing as they galloped after him. Jacob whipped left and leveled his rifle. Now laying down suppressive fire, rounds going wide, it was enough to slow the pack of Reds and force them to take cover. James was at the ridge now, Duke running up the slope ahead of him.

"Move your ass," Rogers yelled.

James looked up at him, panting. "Tha' fuck you think I'm doing?"

Rogers pulled a smoke canister from his belt and threw it into the distance, the canister popping and spewing green smoke to screen James's climb. Jacob moved back into the trees, taking cover behind a tall oak. He bled off the remnants of his magazine, watching another Red fall. Blue plasma raced in his direction, cutting through the smoke and striking precariously close to James as he rolled over the top of the slope.

Rogers reached down and yanked him to his feet. "'Bout time, you lazy bastard. Hope you're up for a run."

"Hell, I thought you'd never ask."

Jacob watched as a formation of armored vehicles rounded the curve of the wall and came into view. He saw the flash as their main guns fired. Jacob dropped back and rolled into the woods, landing on his feet at a full run, the others close behind him. He felt the blast and heat on his back as the forest and ridgeline exploded.

Then it was over. They continued running, crashing through the thick underbelly of the forest, their ears ringing, and their skin burning from the flash burns. At a bend in the contour of the terrain, Rogers led them again uphill, moving them into a draw before heading into a copse of fallen trees. Jacob hurdled over a thick tree, and after several steps dropped into a bed of leaves and pine needles, the adrenaline crash leaving him exhausted. He held the rifle to his chest and hung his head with his mouth wide open, gasping for air.

The others fell in beside him, doing the same. "What the fuck happened back there?" Rogers asked between labored breaths.

James pulled Duke close to him, running his hands along the dog's body, checking it for injuries before rubbing the dog's ears and pouring it a handful of water. "I broke up some sort of ceremony; some flamboyant fucker in a Liberace dress was torturing some old lady. James isn't okay with shit like that. I put him to sleep."

"Yeah, you might have put him to sleep, but you managed to wake up their entire army. Who knows what other damage you caused?" Rogers said.

"It is what it is, but I bet they think twice before doing silly shit like that out in the open again."

Jacob leaned forward, dropping the empty magazine from his rifle before searching for a replacement in his vest. "Did you see anything else?"

James nodded, drying his hand on his trousers. "They got 'em, lots of people in there. It's some kind of town. I was able to get up to a rooftop just across from the orb. They built a fence that runs right around that small town. There are a few houses on the backside that look like they were damaged when that thing landed. For whatever reason, they excluded them from the fence.

"I had a good view of the back approach; something was going on. They positioned all of their guards in and around the orb—had all the civilians marching down the main street for some sort of concert, gathering, or something. I couldn't hear anything, but it must have been important. I was about to pull back and head for the tower when I saw them pull some lady onto the stage. They dumped her head into some of that Delta stew, the black shit that turns them."

"And you stopped it?" Jacob asked.

"He's not in good shape. Popped his grape and put two into his chest."

Rogers grunted. "This isn't good. I think you just poured gas all over the hornets' nest. They'll double up security now and go out in force after us."

James spat and, using a log, drug himself back to his feet. "Wake up, brother, what you think they were already doing? I just let them know they can be touched. I put them on notice. And hell, I plan to do more of it. I just need a bigger gun."

"You might have crushed our only chances of getting inside."

"Damn, Rogers, what the hell are you so afraid of? Look around you. We're fucked. This is all lost already, there's nothing left to lose. I lay up there on that roof watching them, so damn many of them, and not that many of us. The people filed out of those houses, all of them falling in line, doing what they were told to—"

Jacob leaned in. "Did you see Laura?"

The bearded scout shook his head. "No … just crowds of faces all dressed alike. But for the most part they looked safe—except for the one, but she stood up to them. I saw her shout at them before they snatched her from the crowd. Maybe that's what we've got to look forward to. Do what we're told to survive."

"Except they don't accept men into their little commune," Jacob said.

"Wrong, they had men. I watched a couple of them really close. Little rat bastards wearing blue pajamas, like trustees or something, they had more freedom of movement than the others. I was planning to snatch one of the little turncoats. Well, before I saw the Liberace routine."

"We need to go back," Jacob said, having heard enough.

James grinned, swinging his legs over a nearby log. "Now you're talking. But first we need to get back to the tower and rearm."

Chapter 19

The old man lay tucked into thick grass, his eye glued to the scope with a clear sight of the roadblock. He was in an elevated position and less than five hundred meters from the target; they would take several down before they had to withdraw back into the woods. Even if they did not kill them all, it was enough to slow them down, and that was their main objective—to disrupt the enemy movement.

A single alien vehicle blocked the intersection; two Red Sleeves in front, another behind it, one sticking out of the armored turret. The back of the carrier jostled and a ramp dropped, more alien soldiers exiting and moving into the grass alongside the carrier. The ear tickling vibrations stopped as their vehicle shut down and settled onto the surface of the road. These things were settling in for a long shift.

Clem grinned. Excited at the prospects in front of him, he let his hand move to the top of his scope and turned a dial, illuminating a red dot. He steadied the .308 bolt-action rifle and focused on the alien in the turret. He knew more of Matt's soldiers would be farther up the trail, setting improvised explosive devices on the road leading back to the alien base. If these called for help, there would be a surprise for any quick reaction force. They were ready to take the fight back to the enemy. Clem turned his wrist and looked at his watch, almost noon. Almost time to begin.

"Hold up," Masterson whispered.

His spotter was positioned just behind him to his right. He was behind the stock of an M240B machine gun fitted with a long-range scope—a gift from the stores at Emmerson's ridge. "What is it?" Clem asked.

"We got civvies on the road, moving this way."

Clem removed his eye from the scope and squinted into the bright sunlight. He spotted a group of refugees, women and children carrying heavy bags, one with a suitcase on rollers. A sight right out of the Third World. He used his scope to get a better view. Panning left and right, he could only see women; two paced out in front of the others—an elderly woman and a short heavyset woman wrapped in blankets.

The two red-sleeved soldiers at the front of the convoy spread out on the road, watching the approaching mass. One turned back, signaling the alien in the turret. A short moment later, a Gold Sleeve exited the back of the vehicle and joined them on the road. The creature made its way to the front, anticipating, almost welcoming, the approaching civilians.

"They surrendering?" Clem whispered.

"Looks like it. Your call, what do you want to do?"

"I'm hungry, but I'm not eager to take down friendlies in the crossfire," Clem said. "Let's see how this plays out."

As the civilians drew closer, the Gold Sleeve stopped and allowed the Reds to move into position. Clem watched as the Gold opened its arms in a welcoming gesture, waving the women forward, at the same time signaling for the Reds to back away. The guards complied and took a step back, lowering their battle rifles. The civilians hesitated, but continued their march forward.

The Gold slowly approached, her arms outstretched, palms open. A female at the lead of the group stepped forward and stopped when the alien raised her hand. She approached the female and placed a reflective cap atop her head. Almost instantly, the female knelt down to the surface of the road. The Gold nodded and reached into a pouch, retrieving another bowl. It looked up to the next female and waved her forward—the heavyset woman draped in blankets. Two teenaged girls followed close behind, flanking the blanketed woman on both sides.

"I don't like this. I think I'll put a bullet in that little one handing out Yakamas," Clem whispered, allowing the red dot to pan and settle center on the back of the gold-sleeved alien.

Before Masterson could respond, the large woman threw the blanket aside, revealing a snub-nosed revolver. Time seemed to slow as Clem watched the woman's arm extend inches from the gold-sleeved alien's face. The woman pulled the trigger, and the Gold's helmeted head snapped, a puff of red mist exploding from the back. The teen girls on either side drew small hand guns, each unloading into the guards to their fronts.

"Give them cover!" Clem shouted, finally back to his senses. He pivoted hard on his elbows and centered his optic on the alien in the turret. Before he could pull the trigger, the top of the vehicle exploded in bright yellow flames. The alien flailed, its blue-and-red suit engulfed in flame. Clem exhaled and squeezed the trigger, the round tearing through the alien's armor. He heard Masterson's machine gun open up behind him, ripping rounds into the aliens in reserve, cutting them down as they ran forward toward the civilians, making them easy targets in the open and swallowed in the flames of the burning vehicle.

Clem pulled his eye back from the scope, working the bolt as he searched for more targets. He saw the women now scattered across the road front. The rolling suitcase was open, revealing bottles stuffed with rags; the women were showering the vehicle with Molotov cocktails. The heavyset woman stopped over each downed creature, finishing them with a single shot to the head from the revolver while the teen girls swarmed over the dead, removing equipment.

With all of the aliens down, Clem eased off the trigger. He looked to Masterson, who was already on his feet and bounding ahead toward the ambush site. Clem pushed himself to his knees and gathered his equipment. He made another quick scan of the area before moving down, watching the crumpled alien forms as he approached.

The women on the road took notice of the approaching men. The heavyset woman drew a second handgun from her belt and leveled it at Masterson, who quickly put up his hands and slowed his approach. "All on the same side here," Clem shouted, closing the distance. "I'm Clem; this is my buddy, Matt. Mind telling me who you all are?"

The woman lowered her weapon and grabbed the gold-sleeved body by a wrist, straightening its arm. Another female stepped from the back and, using a long blade, slashed down, removing the dead alien's hand.

"What are you doing?" Clem asked.

The woman turned to face him. She stopped and opened what looked like a velvet bag attached to the gold-sleeved creature's hip. She dumped its contents onto the road, the saucer-shaped devices clanging as they spilled out. "These are some type of mind-control devices. Only a guide's hand can remove it once it's in place." She pointed as another woman used the dead alien's hand to remove the saucer from the elderly woman's head.

"Guides?" Masterson asked.

The women quickly circled back around the blanketed woman, the teen girls holding bags stuffed with goods, the roller suitcase now re-filled with the alien rifles. She looked at Clem and Masterson then down at a stopwatch hanging around her neck. "I'd be happy to speak to you, but we have to get off the road. They'll have called for backup by now."

An explosion roared from the north. Clem turned to see a mushroom cloud forming over the distant trees. "We were ready for their back up," Clem said. "Mind telling me who you all are now?"

Before she could answer, an open-backed pickup truck raced onto the road from somewhere in the woods. The women quickly tossed their goods into the back and piled in.

"You can call me Ruth," she said, tossing her blankets into the truck and pulling herself into the back.

"Now you all coming or just going to stand here with your thumbs up your ass?" the woman shouted.

Chapter 20

The man's heart still raced in a panicked frenzy; he stood by the window, looking out into a street filled with soldiers. Transports roared over the surface, surrounded by scores of the witnesses; no longer apathetic, they were now active and enraged. *The high council will not stand for this. They will be out for vengeance and looking for someone to punish.* He looked at the defiant woman he had been assigned. *Why this one?* he thought, dropping his head. *Why not one of the more subservient wives from the refugee camps who were eager for a fresh bed and comfort?*

"What have your people done?" Francis said, eyeing the woman standing stoically behind a kitchen counter. He saw the smug expression on her face, the lack of understanding in her eyes.

Laura laughed defiantly. "*My people*? Are you no longer part of the human race?"

"What was it you said when the Messenger was killed?" he asked.

She pursed her lips and looked away.

"It was something about rejection; do you know what this act of defiance will mean to the community?" Francis turned away, pulling the heavy drapes closed. "There is so much you don't understand; so much that *your people* don't understand. If they only knew, they would stop these senseless attacks."

She ignored him, moved to the refrigerator, retrieving a pitcher of water, and filled a plastic cup, slowly locking eyes on the locked front door. He caught her gaze and followed it. *What is wrong with this woman? Why can she not see the comfort and safety the community provides?*

"Don't even think about running, especially not now. They would kill you for sure. They won't be able to hold back the soldiers. The entire council will be out for blood tonight," he said. *And my blood with it when they discover my failure with this one.*

"Why are you here, Francis? Why us? Why can't you take a different family of prisoners?"

Oh my dear, how I wish I had a choice. Francis shook his head and moved away from the window. Walking around the sofa, he sighed and sat heavily on the overstuffed cushions. He shrugged before leaning his head back. "Again, I am not a guard and you are not a prisoner."

Laura forced a smug laugh. "So I can leave then? You won't try to stop me?"

"You're safe here." He clenched his fist, letting it rest on his thigh. She was lucky he did not believe in the practices of some of the other mentors. It was probably his French upbringing, his reluctance to violence, and maybe the distant thoughts of his own mother long gone. Besides, she was a strong woman and Francis knew that barbaric methods would not work to win her over.

"I'm a prisoner. And you didn't answer my question. Why us?" Laura asked, her tone changing.

"I was assigned to you. I am your mentor."

"Who assigned you?"

"The Creators, of course. We never know why; it is just the way." *I wish I knew. What did I do to deserve this?*

Laura looked away and left the room, taking the water and walking the hallway to a small bedroom. Francis followed her, keeping his distance. Katy was asleep. He watched as she lifted the blankets around the girl and tucked them in, leaving the cup on a nightstand. He turned to the window and saw the ominous shadows moving past the drawn curtains. He watched as Laura moved to the glass and drew back the curtain then pulled back upon seeing the witnesses walking a silent sentry around the homes in the neighborhood.

He stiffened his jaw. “They are for our protection,” Francis said quietly from behind her, trying to sound reassuring.

“Protection? Or to keep me from leaving or from talking to the neighbors,” Laura protested. She turned and edged past him back into the living room, stopping in front of the door. Francis sighed and followed close behind her. He watched as she put her hand on the knob. “What would happen if I walked outside and went next door?”

Francis shrugged, knowing she would be killed before she reached the street. Maybe he should let her; end this struggle and take his chances with the council. “And why would you want to do that?”

She shook her head at him in frustration. He could see tears welling at the corners of her eyes—she was breaking.

“I don’t know … to borrow a cup of sugar. What does it matter?!” she said, her voice rising.

“I can send for anything you need; within reason, of course.”

With that, Laura finally burst into tears, her frustration peaking. He approached her, but she turned away and put up a hand. “Don’t even,” she shouted.

Francis backed away with his hands at his sides, his face showing sympathy but his mind smiling; this woman that put up the strong front was finally breaking. “You just don’t understand.”

“Then explain it to me,” she shouted. “Why are they here?”

Francis frowned and turned his back to her, smiling when she could not see. He took several steps before pausing to look back. “They may kill us all for what happened today. That’s the law if a community turns against a Messenger,” Francis said wearily before moving to the dining table and sitting. He folded his hands in front of him and looked down. It was the first time he had allowed Laura to see real emotion from him, and not the optimistic look of an infomercial sales clerk. He would have to use this opportunity to bring her into the fold.

“If that’s the law, then why are we still alive?” she asked.

He would have to plan every word. Every bit would have to draw her in to convince her that their path was the only way and anything else would mean death or a life of suffering. “They are in session. Our only hope is that the elders consider this an outside attack and not from within the walls of the communal," Francis said in a low voice while looking down at his hands. "Might I bother you for some tea? You'll find it in the pantry." A simple request, would she oblige him?

Laura nodded and opened the cabinet door, removing a covered tin filled with tea bags. As she retrieved the kettle from the stove and filled it, she asked, "Who are the council?"

Francis sighed and looked up at her with serious eyes. "They are everything," he said, the pitch of the salesman gone from his voice. "I've never seen them. I never will. They never come down." He was not lying; in all the years he had been in the community, he'd never been allowed an audience with the Creators.

As far as Francis knew, they never visited the terrestrial planet and always stayed hidden from human eyes. He looked at her and pondered if she was ready and would be able to accept the truth should he tell her. There were arguments among the council that only children should be taken. It had been their way for centuries. Adults were deemed incompatible with the knowledge and would not accept the message; they were too old, too stubborn even, and their world views already coded.

But this was a migration and if the communities were to succeed, they would have to take in everyone. At some point an agreement was made; a worker class would be needed and they couldn't wait for a generation of children to come of age. The compromise was to accept women, mothers, with the reasoning that they would sacrifice for their offspring and willingly join the community.

"To Earth, you mean?" Laura asked.

Francis nodded; he would try. "Yes. Laura, I know this all sounds strange to you, unbelievable even, but they have been here long before any of us. Your indigenous people probably felt the same when they saw the first white man. But, you shouldn't fear them; they don't consider themselves guests or invaders. In their eyes, this is not our planet. It is theirs. They have invested in it, and *we* are the guests."

"Guests?" Laura asked, moving to the table with the kettle and two small cups.

Francis thought for a moment. "Guest is the wrong word. Children, maybe … or extended family left to occupy a residence. But they're back now, and they aren't happy with the way we've taken care of their home, the path we have taken. This was their planet and meant to be their home."

She poured the hot water over a tea bag, filling the mug, and slid it across the table. Francis lifted it and teased the string, dunking the bag into the steaming liquid. He lifted the mug to his lips and took a cautious sip before setting it back in front of him. "They've been here many times—many, many times over the ages. They planted the seeds, passively guided us, kick-started our development, and tracked our progress. All the signs of their visits were there if people had bothered to look. They are much older than us, you know. Their written history dates back to before the dinosaurs.

"When they first visited, they found a place that is only a shell of what it is today. Over a thousand years ago they started the exodus plan with hopes that when their planet died, ours would be ready for their arrival; that our people and technology would be ready for them."

"A thousand years ago?" Laura asked.

"That was what they call 'the beginning'. The first time a Messenger stepped foot on our planet and chose to intervene in our development, they formed their first outpost in the depths of a cave and used it to explore and examine our ways. The Messengers found us to be violent and disgusting creatures. Earth was rejected by the council and it was determined the planet was not ready for their arrival.

"This is why they first came to live among us. It was a small presence then; only a Messenger and a few guides to show us the way. A small human tribe was chosen and their leader given the truth. The first time they shared their message, they started a following that grew and spread quickly. That should have put us on the correct path to paradise; instead, our species resisted and failed to come together. Most of the populous rejected the message and it led to wars with the tribes that failed to follow us.

"Don't you understand? The Messengers guided us in the hope we would build a great society that they could one day join. They did not want to destroy us. However, we failed to evolve in time; we are still living as hundreds, even thousands, of tribes under many banners. The Creators have run out of time. Their planet is dying and they can no longer wait for us to grow into a harmonious society. Now they have come to correct the wrongs of our way, and they will not stop until it is complete. Those that have taken witness have ensured this."

"Witness? Why do you call them that?"

"They have been given the truth; it shows them the way and has made them genetically superior—"

"It kills them. I've seen what it does, it took away my friends and neighbors," she blurted out.

"The truth saves them, improves everything about them, and brings them into the communal in a way we could never comprehend."

Laura looked away, clenching a fist and watching the shadows pass by the kitchen windows. "Then why were we spared from it?"

"Every civilization must make sacrifices to advance; the witnesses made that sacrifice for us. They have been granted the true potential of our race. You think of them as dead but they aren't … they now live in full connection with the Creator," Francis said, looking up at the ceiling. "One day, they will be far greater than any of us."

Laura scowled. "Is this just religious indoctrination, an interstellar cult? All of this is sounding more and more like a galactic holy war."

Maybe she wasn't ready, he thought. "You mustn't speak that way. It's blasphemy."

"Blasphemy? You know we won't stop, that we won't stop fighting—wait, of course, you do know, don't you? That's why you've separated us from our men."

"The soldiers have declared your men dangerous. Your men attacked us," Francis said with sincerity.

"Attacked? Who are you, Francis? How did they get you?"

Thunder cracked in the distance and rain began to tap against the roof. Francis grinned and leaned back in his chair. *Maybe she understands more than she lets on.* "I am not important. You shouldn't think in the ways of individuals. It will only prevent you from seeing the truth. We are a community; we must do what's good for the community."

Laura bit her lower lip, ignoring his statement. "Where the hell are you from? They've been here less than a week, yet you talk like you've known them your entire life."

Francis grinned, thinking to his first days in the community as a child; a day when he was extracted from the burning rubble of a bombed city, tanks rumbling in the distance. How the Messengers took him in and showed him the way. His face broke into a smile. "Because I have been with them my entire life."

Chapter 21

Rain pounded and soaked through his uniform top. They patroled in a column with James leading the way, winding a path up the steep hillside toward the radio tower just visible in the distance. Lightning flashed, exposing bits of the darkened trail in strobes of uneven light. He couldn't get his mind off the walled community and the people inside. His heart told him Laura was there, and he wanted nothing more than to return. Looking ahead, he saw Rogers and James. He knew they wouldn't steer him wrong; he had to trust them as he always had.

James paused at the end of the thick woods. Kneeling, he let his eyes pan over the clearing ahead and pointed to a lone grassy hilltop barely visible in the low light. The steel bunker door cut into the hillside was barely visible between the flashes of light. "You think the others made it up here?" Jacob whispered.

Rogers shrugged. "Someone did and they made a half-assed attempt at camouflaging the door with brush. I wonder who? Only one way to—"

"Wait," James whispered, extending an arm to ease them back into cover. He waved and pointed down the trail before ducking back into the brush.

Jacob followed the scout's gloved hand and saw them: three tall Red Sleeves leading a fourth and shorter Gold along the muddy trail that led to the radio tower. The aliens moved through a clearing of high grass, following the trail toward them at an angle. Jacob knew from the previous trip that the trail would disappear in a bend before traveling past where he now stood. The two Reds stalked out front, leading the way, with the Gold in the middle, and the other Red following farther back.

Jacob crouched in the heavy brush and raised his rifle, taking aim. Rogers reached over and squeezed the hand guard of his M4, shaking his head side to side. "No guns. We fire up here and they'll be all over us." Rogers released his grip on the rifle and pulled a fighting knife from a scabbard on his chest. James smiled and quietly slipped across the trail before ducking into cover.

Jacob searched his belt, looking for his own knife. Rogers looked back at him and whispered, "Let them pass. We'll take the lead two, and you take down the one in the rear. We need this to be quiet."

Jacob nodded. "And the Gold?"

"We'll handle that one last. It doesn't appear armed, maybe it's wounded," he said.

Jacob tipped his head in Rogers's direction and watched him slip away. He then did the same. Squatting and slipping back into the wet foliage, he allowed himself to blend with his surroundings completely before the alien patrol emerged from the cover of the bend. Jacob's heart rate quickened as the first of the Reds moved past his hiding spot.

He could hear the creak of the alien's uniform, flexing and squeaking in the rain like polished leather. The thought distracted him. *It wouldn't be leather unless the aliens had cows, or is any hide leather?* The aliens' helmets emitted a soft glow of light where they fit over the creatures' heads. Jacob wondered if they had special optics like night vision and thermals. *They must,* he told himself. *They're advanced. But if they do, then why haven't they spotted us? Or maybe they have and it's all a trap, maybe they planned all of this.* Another moved past, and finally the smaller Gold figure slowly neared Jacob's position.

Jacob sat perfectly still, allowing the cool rain to flow over his body and the damp leaves to shield his form against the wood line. *No, maybe it's the rain. That's why they can't see us; it must mess up their optics.* Before he could finish his thought, a low hum emitted from the lead creature. The others halted and raised their rifles. Jacob watched the Gold step ahead, moving closer to those in the lead while the one in the rear turned to face the trail behind it. *Just as a trained soldier would,* he thought.

He froze, watching the tail Red's head pan and scan the tree line, sure that it would turn and spot him less than five yards away. *They couldn't have seen me. If they did they would have already fired. Maybe it's a proximity sensor then, just something that detects, but doesn't pinpoint ... I guess that's possible. No more impossible than aliens landing in giant pumpkins.*

Jacob heard a growl followed by several barks. He watched as the Gold took a startled step back. The scout dog was on the trail now, in a fighter's stance. Duke showed his teeth and growled, the hair standing stiff on the dog's back. A Red squared off curiously, the humming became louder, and he raised his rifle. From nowhere, streaks and blurs of multi-cam crossed the trail followed by a flash of steel and a spray of blood.

Jacob remembered what he was supposed to be doing. He forced himself forward, springing from bent knees to explode onto the trail and colliding with the far larger creature in a footballer's tackle. The creature ducked and tried to roll Jacob off. A fatal mistake. It was at the wrong angle, and Jacob was able to curl his arm around the thing's neck and sink his blade just under the alien's helmet. The crunch of bone and the tearing of sinew vibrated through the knife as the blade struck home. The creature collapsed while its wet sticky blood warmed Jacob's gloved hand.

Jacob hit the ground hard and continued his forward roll into the grass, somehow finding his way to his knees, his rifle slapping against his side from the sling. He looked up and saw the Gold staring at him. It pointed its golden-gloved left fist in Jacob's direction. Seeing him on his knees, helpless and only feet away with the bloodied knife, the creature hesitated. Things moved quickly; Jacob sat stunned, looking at the creature that he was sure shared his own sense of shock.

The dog's continued growling, joined by a noise from up the trail, forced the creature to look away and into the direction of the sound. Rogers and James were slowly approaching with their rifles held up, the crumpled bodies of the red-sleeved soldiers lying dead at their feet.

"Take it easy there, Gold Finger," James said, moving ahead and leading the way with his rifle's barrel.

The Gold stiffened, its head shifting from Jacob to James while its gloved hand moved along with its head. It stopped on James and pointed a gold finger.

"Now, I ain't sure what it is you got going on with that fancy glove, but where I come from it ain't friendly to point," James said.

The alien curled its finger, gracefully retracted its hand, and then removed its helmet. James's jaw dropped as his head leaned back, his eyes squinting in the low light. The creature revealed a soft feminine face. Perfectly shaped and formed like the finest porcelain doll. Rain pelted off its smooth hairless head, water running down and over high cheek bones. The alien lowered its arm and rested the helmet on its hip. She blinked wide eyes and spoke in a smooth female voice. "I submit; I am yours to do with as you wish."

James stammered, taken aback by the alien's appearance and soft-spoken words. He sarcastically shook his head then exhaled loudly, regaining his senses. "Oh no, this isn't the first time I've had a pretty gal tell me that. Never ends well for me, usually passed out and naked with all my credit cards gone."

"Cover and bind it," Rogers said. Stomping forward, he slapped a pair of zip ties in James's hand.

Jacob watched as the bearded scout nodded and yanked a bit of cloth from his belt. He grabbed the slender alien by the shoulders and spun it around, blindfolding it. He took its right wrist and bound it with a zip tie, but before he could wrap the left wrist, the hand opened, revealing a flash of light. James's arm's stiffened, and he convulsed while falling back. Rogers was still close. He swung hard, catching the creature in the solar plexus with the butt of his rifle.

The alien reeled, releasing James from his agony. The creature turned, now trying to direct its weapon at Rogers. Before it could, the soldier stomped down heavily on the outside of the alien's knee, forcing it down, while Rogers threw a forearm to direct the alien's weapon up and away. The creature let out a screeching gasp as it fell into the thick mud.

Rogers moved by the crumpled form and kicked its ankles so that they were close together. With his boot on the thing's back, he squatted low and grabbed the creature's gloved wrist then twisted it so hard Jacob thought it may snap. Unable to remove the weaponized glove, he used a roll of tape and made several passes to get the tape to stick in the pouring rain. He wrapped the gloved hand into a fist before binding it to the other then taped the creature's arms to its waist. "Try that again and I cut the hand off," he said.

Rogers then eased back and taped the ankles together. He leaned down and easily hoisted the now restrained creature to his shoulder. James was still recovering on the ground, sitting up wide eyed and forcing an embarrassed smile to his face. "You okay?" Rogers asked.

"They get me every damn time," he chuckled.

"Give it a rest! It isn't even human," Rogers spat. "Get off your ass; we need to move."

Jacob smirked and extended a hand, pulling James back to his feet; the scout stood and slapped the wet mud from his pants. "What about them?" Jacob said, pointing to the dead.

White lights came on in the far distance, emitting a soft glow that outlined the hilltop and backlit the radio tower.

"Leave 'em, there's no time," Rogers said, already moving toward the bunker door. Crossing the remaining distance at a near jog, Jacob followed Rogers's lead, with James lagging behind still recovering from the stun. The bunker door was partially concealed by cut limbs and pine boughs, but not enough to completely hide it. Rogers moved past it to the sloping hill and dropped the creature hard to the ground. He spun back to Jacob. "Keep an eye on it."

Jacob nodded and moved toward the crumpled form and knelt down with his rifle close to his chest. He watched James move in and take a position across from the door with Duke by his side. Rogers worked his way through the cover of the brush and tapped lightly on the door before lifting a latch and swinging the door in. A low rectangle of light cut out and Rogers turned back. “Get inside, now.”

Chapter 22

The building was old; exposed rough-cut planks covered with heavy coats of paint reflected back the soft glow of gas lanterns. High industrial rafters were covered with webs and stained with dust and smoke from a hundred years' worth of fires. Clem let his eyes adjust as he searched the open space, noting the walls were covered with block and tackle, and rusted hooks wound with heavy rope hung from the ceiling. In the back, he could barely make out a group of people huddled around wooden tables lit low by candlelight, the flickering flames silhouetting the mass of people.

He could smell the wood smoke and a faint scent of roasting meat. People spoke in hushed tones. A vehicle door slammed and he heard the husky woman's commanding voice behind him. "Leave your gear against the wall; you can hold onto your rifles," she said as she stomped past him.

Masterson followed her then stopped by Clem's side. "What do you think?"

Clem dipped his chin. "Do what she says; maybe there's a hot meal in it for us," he said, tossing his rucksack to the side. When the others were out of earshot, he turned to Masterson and whispered, "We need whatever intel these people can give us."

Masterson shrugged and stepped off, following the others toward the candlelit corner. Faces slowly materialized around the table. Four women—their hair pulled back and wearing dark clothing, army surplus jackets, and ill-fitted hunting parkas—were hovering over a road map covered with push pins.

A red-haired woman looked up at Clem, scowled, and turned to Ruth. "Who are the strays?" she asked.

"Found them on the road. I didn't think they would make it through the night on their own," Ruth said.

Clem grunted; the red-haired woman looked at him then back to Ruth. "How'd it go?"

Ruth moved around the table and ran a hand across the map, pointing a finger at a long stretch of road. "Here," she said, taking a pin and pressing it into the map. "We wrecked one of their trucks and a squad of their soldiers. No casualties on our side."

The woman raised her eyebrows. "Any of the little ones?"

Ruth nodded. "Yeah, you were right about them; they're still eager to take us in. Whatever has them spun up, it hasn't stopped them from wanting prisoners. We stopped in the road like you told us and that thing came right out to greet us."

The red-haired woman showed no emotion; she looked back at Clem and Masterson. "And what's the story with these two?"

Ruth scowled. "They were up in the weeds—watching us, I guess. They seemed useful and didn't get in the way so I brought them back."

"Useful? Ha! Hell, if we hadn't been up there, they would have cut you down," Clem said. "You can't hit an up-armed patrol with hand guns and liquor bottles."

"My ass! You put us in danger; my girls had it handled."

Clem laughed at that and moved closer to the table. Looking behind him, he found an old wooden chair and pulled it close before sitting down.

"Go on … make yourself at home," Ruth scowled.

Ignoring her, he leaned forward and stared down at the map. "So, what have we got here?"

The red-haired woman looked him over then let her eyes drift to Masterson, her gaze stopping at his weapons and equipment. "I've seen enough soldiers in my time to know you're either military or one of those veteran militia crazies. Which is it?" she asked.

"Which would you prefer?" Clem said.

"Mister, whoever you are, we don't have time for games." She turned and whispered to one of the younger girls positioned around the table. The young girl, barely a teen, nodded then moved back, disappearing to the left.

Masterson stepped out of the shadows and stood over Clem's shoulder. "Military, ma'am. Excuse our manners; we've been on the run since those things showed up. We were prepping to ambush the group on the road when your party came along."

"So you haven't followed the call to surrender like the rest of them?"

Masterson looked down at her curiously. "Surrender, ma'am?"

She turned back to a radio. "A man has been on the radio broadcasting a looped message. He claims they've negotiated peace. Said all of the military units were being stood down. If we drop our weapons and come in peacefully that these things—friends he called them—would take care of us."

"Anything else?" Clem asked.

She nodded. "They claim we are the aggressors now; that they have come in peace and we attacked them."

Masterson shook his head and looked to Clem before looking back to the red-haired woman. "Honestly, this is the first I've heard of any surrender. As far as I'm concerned, my boys will fight until they don't have any fight left in them," he said.

She nodded curtly, looked at the map, and pointed a finger. "Okay then, so how many in your command? Where are they? We need supplies."

"I'm sorry; I dissolved what was left of my company yesterday."

"Then you did surrender," she snapped back.

"No, ma'am; just sent them underground so they could cause more damage. I assure you they are doing what they can to slow down the enemy."

The young girl returned to the table, holding a notepad. She handed it to the red-haired woman, who flipped through pages cautiously before stopping at one then set the notebook on the table. "Toronto is completely lost. They have the city surrounded; only unarmed civilians are being allowed to enter."

Clem cleared his throat and spoke up, answering for Masterson. "Before we get into all of this Q and A, how about you tell us who you are and what you're all doing here?"

She smiled and pulled up a chair of her own. "They call me the Grandmother, and this is the resistance."

"Resistance?" Clem said, trying to keep a smile from his face.

"Mister, I'm sure you can find humor in this, but after they showed up, things changed. All of our men are gone; the camps aren't safe anymore. While the military has been doing whatever it is you do, those things were going from town to town, killing every man standing against them and taking the rest away. Most of the camps, and some of the cites, are completely occupied now."

"Wait, what do you mean taking the rest away?" Masterson asked. "Taking them where?"

The woman lifted the notepad and shook the small book. "We think we know where, but what we don't know is why. Most of us came from the city before it was sealed off; some of us from the camps to the south. Those things came in after the first of the bombs dropped on the cities and military bases. Then they waited … they used the black eyes to corral us, and then they started capturing. I was with my husband and two daughters when they cornered us on the road. We tried to surrender …"

"What happened?" Masterson asked.

"One of their soldiers executed my husband then one of the small gold ones did something to us, and we couldn't move. They put my girls in their truck … I would be gone too if Ruth and her people hadn't come along."

Ruth grunted. "It wasn't nothin' heroic … completely by accident. We were running the same as the rest. We'd just been attacked west of Toronto after the first of the bombs dropped and had been driving through the night when we saw Sarah lying on the road and those things standing over her. They took her girls and were about to take her too. We just did what we could; started shooting. I guess it was enough because they pulled back and let us be."

Masterson nodded. "How many of you are there?"

Ruth frowned. "We had a lot more yesterday—I lost a lot just finding this place. We were out looking for survivors when we ran into their patrol."

"So your attack on their convoy today, that was spontaneous?"

"We try to keep patrols out around the clock," she said, motioning to pins on the map. "Our priority is to find survivors before they do. But, if given the opportunity, we kill them."

"And you think you know where they are taking them?" Masterson asked.

Sarah nodded and held up the notebook. "One of the women we brought in this morning knows where a dome landed. She said their soldiers were walking survivors on the road toward it. More are being guided that way by the hour. We have contact with all of the militias in the area; they are ready to strike when we give the word."

Masterson looked down at Clem beside him. "We need to get eyes on this thing and find out if maybe there's a way to hurt it. How soon could your people be ready to attack?"

A door opened and a pair of women dressed in fatigues carrying pump-action shotguns filed into the open room. "Ruth, they're here," one said, alarm showing in her voice.

"How many?"

The girl shook her head. “There’s a lot of them this time; way more than before. I don’t know if they’ve seen us, but their numbers are growing.”

“What’s going on?” Clem asked.

Ruth looked away from the girls and locked eyes with Clem. “The Black Eyes—they found us.”

Chapter 23

With dawn came an eerie calm as the rain beating on the roof soothed her. The storm continued, its thunder blocking the dark thoughts in her head. Laura tossed the thick comforter away and left the bed. She cautiously crept the hallway, fully expecting to see Francis still there, but he was gone. The kitchen was clean, and the door closed. On closer inspection, she could see that he'd left it unbolted. She did not know if that was a show of trust, or a test, or possibly a complete loss of faith in her.

Laura approached to the door and pulled away the heavy curtain that covered the glass pane set in the top. She saw two women standing alone at the end of the sidewalk. They were dressed head to toe in black, only their bald heads exposed. Laura eyed them suspiciously. The women stood in place until they were joined by others then they turned toward the door and navigated the sidewalk in Laura's direction.

She backed away, put her hand on the lock, and felt the sweat building in her palm. When she looked back up, she could see a dark-faced woman standing just outside the door. She heard the knock and before it could register, she saw her hands open the door. The woman stepped into the opening and inspected her, her head slowly panning over her body. The woman reached for Laura's wrists. Her hands were cold and dry as she turned Laura's palms up and inspected them.

"You'll come with us now," the woman said with an accent the Laura had never heard.

"But my daughter … I'm not even dressed," she protested.

The woman waved a hand and two women brushed through the doorway, quickly draping Laura in a dark gown and heavy cloak; another woman crouched and placed a leather slipper on each foot. When they finished with her, they nudged her forward.

"Your child will attend school, you will come with us," the woman said.

"Where is Francis? I want to talk to him," she said.

From the back, another leathery skinned woman marched forward and scowled at Laura. She looked her up and down and gritted her teeth in disappointment. "Why always the lazy ones?" she muttered before looking Laura in the eye. The leathered woman held a small chrome box and smiled at Laura as she caressed the box in her palm. Laura felt a static sensation in the plate on her head.

"The Creator does not demand obedience … he expects it," she said.

"And if I ref—?" Laura felt a quick squeezing sensation in her head that subsided as quickly as it came, the world going light then dark as if a light switch had been flipped. She looked back up at the leather-faced woman.

The woman glared back. "Any more questions?"

Laura shook her head *no*, a tear forming in the corner of her eye; she wanted to show strength, but she felt broken, her head still cloudy from the pressure. The woman showed no mercy and nodded to the others. They formed around Laura and pressed her out of the house and onto the walkway.

Not speaking, the women guided her to the street where others huddled around her in the pouring rain. She tried to turn her head but lost sight of the leathered woman. At the next house, she was forced to wait in the street as another woman was retrieved. She now understood the group she stood with were all new like her. This was their common bond; instead of resisting the huddle, she now fell into it. Hands clapped and the group shuffled along moving quickly now. Laura recognized the course and knew they were returning to the orb.

They were stopped and formed into a straight line, standing shoulder to shoulder. Laura looked up and saw men dressed in the same dark blue as Francis moving from a hatch in the Orb. She watched them until a firm hand squeezed the back of her neck and she heard the leathered woman's voice. "Do not look at them." She spoke louder so the others could hear. "Do not speak to them."

Laura focused her eyes to the ground as a man paced by her, stopped, and faced her before stepping off. She was then led forward; looking left and right, she saw she was now in a new line along with five others.

The leathered woman was replaced by a frail woman in an identical dark robe who said, "Come, this way."

Following the instructions and moving ahead, Laura saw that the others had already begun to follow so she fell in close to the group, moving toward the hatch. She watched as the blue-dressed men moved in ahead of them, vanishing in the opening. Soon they were on the ramp, climbing up toward the opening, the metallic surface scuffing against the soft sole of their sandals. She heard a woman whimper, sobbing quietly as another tried to comfort her. The woman guiding them ignored their agony, walking straight ahead as they followed.

The hatch was rough, the surface appearing old and unmaintained. Laura tried to look inside, but the interior was dimly lit. The ramp faded into the floor of the space that was a rough metallic, the walls made of the identical material. Laura expected pneumatic hatches and sliding doors, laser lights and soft hospital-like lighting. Instead, what she found was very industrial; the space was rough and soot covered. Carved into the walls were symbols that looked vaguely familiar—like hieroglyphics, but instead of cranes and alligators, they were strange creatures.

The passageway narrowed and they were squeezed into two columns of three. The space smelled smoky and oily, like the belly of an ocean vessel. None of it was what she expected of an alien space craft. Finally, they rounded a corner that ended at another rough-cut wall. Laura tried to search for anything useful, but the lights were low and all she found was a space void of any recognizable features. A crunching sound of gears and the wall began to move up. Lights flickered, casting the space in a dizzying strobe effect.

The robed woman guided them into what appeared to be a large kitchen. They stripped off the soaked cloaks and hung them along a row of hooks evenly spaced high on the wall. Other women in black garbs were already hard at work removing food from pots and setting up plates on shiny metallic trays, some containing bowls, others with pitchers and glasses. The stench made her choke, and she fought back the revulsion.

Laura and the others were again formed into a line standing shoulder to shoulder, facing the kitchen staff. The last of the bowls were filled and the kitchen staff was formed into lines and marched back through the same hatch Laura's group had just entered.

The robed woman moved in front of them; she turned her head to verify they were alone. "I am Taurine; you now answer to me. You will serve the guides their afternoon meal. You will not speak to them. You will follow any and all instructions. If you violate any of the rules of our order, you will be witnessed." The woman paused. "Do you understand?" Her voice was calmer and more reassuring than the leathered woman's.

Laura nodded as the woman panned, examining their faces. "Each day will be better than the next."

The back wall made a grating sound and slid to the left, revealing an open dining room filled with the humanoid creatures dressed in gold linen. They were seated around long communal tables. Consumed in conversation, they didn't bother to look up or seem to notice the dingy kitchen filled with servants.

Taurine stepped forward and gently touched Laura's wrist. "You serve the mélange," she said, pointing to a tray of glasses. Without waiting for a response, Taurine moved on assigning other responsibilities to the women.

Nervous, Laura bit her lower lip and stepped forward cautiously. She edged to the metallic counter and gripped the tray in both hands. She noticed the glasses had already been filled and the carafe was topped off as well. The tray was heavy so she held it close to her body to stabilize its weight. She turned toward the open dining room and saw some of the seated guides eye her impatiently.

She moved ahead; the room filled with sounds of alien voices, her knowledge plate struggling to keep up while processing several conversations at once, and her head filled with waves of strange conversations that made no sense to her. She stepped lightly alongside a table, her legs feeling heavy and wobbly, the tray rattled in her grasp.

She moved between a pair of seated guides; one reached up without making eye contact and casually grabbed a glass, the one across from her doing the same. She proceeded to move away when the closest guide snarled at her, took the carafe, and placed it in the center of the table then shooed her away with a flick of its wrist. Laura inhaled deeply, trying to calm her nerves and moved on. Looking around, she could see the other women were now all holding trays and making their way around the room.

The fact that the guides seemed to have no interest in them helped her to relax. She tried to not focus on the job of serving and instead take in the sights of the room for anything useful, anything she could use. She strained her eyes, trying to look up and into her mind and silence the storm of voices, tuning in and out of several conversations until one caught her attention.

"The council is not happy with the Messenger's loss."

"Do you know who will replace him?"

"No, but when he arrives, the retribution will be delivered. They have chosen to spare the community and instead will hit the outside harshly. It appears the local resistance is not isolated, so the migration here is not going well."

"How so?"

"The other settlements are far ahead of this one. The council will not tolerate our ineffectiveness

and our sustained losses ... We have to be ready for exodus ..."

"You there!" a voice echoed loudly in her head.

Laura suddenly realized she had stopped moving and her tray was still resting in her hands while she'd been lost in the voices inside her head.

"Yes, you," she heard again over the others. Laura glanced down and saw a female face—the same as the one she'd met on her arrival. Scanning the room, she saw they all looked identical in every way, only a scar or birthmark to tell them apart.

Laura began to speak but held her tongue in fear of the warning she'd received. Her hands gripped the tray tightly, and she stared down at her white knuckles, afraid she may have already offended the alien by looking it in the eyes.

"It's okay, you may speak to me," the guide said.

Laura looked up again, waiting for a response.

"Has every guest been served?" the guide asked.

Laura again eyed down. "I'm sorry."

"Do not be sorry, be obedient. Do not stand and wait to be called," the guide said, shooing her away.

Laura backed away and hurriedly completed her rounds around the table before returning to the kitchen with an empty tray. She set it on the counter then pressed her palms onto the cold metallic surface, listening to her heart beat.

Taurine watched as she put back her head and took deep breaths. The old woman moved by her side. "Why are you in distress? Why do you find it difficult to serve the communal, what is there to fear?" she asked.

Laura felt the presence of the others—the women returning to the kitchens with empty trays of their own. They gathered around her, all looking at Taurine.

"This is not a trick or a difficult question; you may answer it freely," Taurine said. "I am here to help you with the transition."

Laura gaped at her confused. "What transition?"

"Is that why you are afraid?" Taurine asked. "Because of the unknowns?"

Laura pursed her lips. “It’s because everything has been taken from me.”

“Everything? Do you not have a daughter? A home? A purpose?” The woman waved her arms, motioning the kitchen. “What more would you need?”

Laura fought to hold back her emotions. “What about my husband?” she said, her voice breaking and a tear forming at the corner of her eye.

“You’ve been assigned a mate; does Francis not suit you?”

Laura gasped and looked away.

Taurine flashed a wicked smile. “Oh, you didn’t know. Well then, maybe *you* are the one that is not being found suitable. I suggest you work on that before you are cast aside. Do you think that would be best for your child?”

The old woman clapped her hands, bringing the other women in close. The door to the dining room slid closed as a new group of women entered the space from behind them. Laura listened as they were given instructions on what their job would be. She leered up and locked eyes with Taurine, who flashed her a vindictive smile.

“You are all dismissed. Your mates will greet you in the passageway,” Taurine said.

Laura stumbled and stepped toward the exit door, her body feeling heavy and out of breath. She moved slowly, falling into the group of women. She wanted to be far away from the vindictive woman who appeared to take pleasure in her agony. She fell into line, following the others through the narrow opening and back into the dimly lit passageway. Just as Taurine had said, she found Francis there waiting for her.

He didn't speak, turning away once she acknowledged him, knowing that she had no choice but to follow.

Chapter 24

The bunker didn't spare them from the sounds of the roaring storm outside its walls. The space was cold and dreary; rain seeped under the door, turning the concrete a dark gray. A stream of murky water traced a line between the tired soldiers, making its way to a drain vent located in the center of the small space. The man-made cavern was dimly lit by a single low-watt bulb hanging in the center of the bunker.

Jacob watched Jesse move, happy to see him on his feet. His friend was back; the attack had invigorated him. He stood in the corner over a propane stove warming water for soup. His neck still wore a bandage, and his body bore the wounds from the fight, but he knew the other soldiers expected more from him as a scout, and he was doing his best to put on a show.

Not designed for housing, the bunker was filled to capacity. Along with the two who came in with Jesse, four more had arrived during the night. Survivors and stragglers, men who, when they found the destroyed cabin, knew this was the last refuge in the area. Along the floor, intermixed with bundles of equipment and crates, men sat exhausted. A lone soldier stationed himself at the back, fidgeting with the only working radio, desperate for a signal. All the landlines back to the cabin were dead; an uplink to the radio tower was their only hope.

Jacob pressed against his space of open wall, moving his knees to keep them from the encroaching water. His eyes turned and focused on the prisoner across from him. Its head was still covered in the fabric, its wrists and ankles still bound, and the blue-and-gold-sleeved uniform coated with mud from the trail. Rogers and James were arguing about what to do with it, how and whether or not to interrogate it. The other men listened in anxiously, this being the first live alien they'd managed to capture.

"We need to get that uniform off and get rid of it," James said. "It could have a tracker embedded in it; they're probably using it to find us right now."

Rogers rubbed his forehead wearily. "Seems like they'd already be on us if that was the case."

James pointed up at the ceiling. "These walls are pretty thick and shielded by the cell company that originally built it. Who knows how much shielding our guys added to it? Probably blocking the signal." He paused and stared at the alien in deep thought before nodding. "Yeah, it's got a tracker. Hell, I bet they're out there right now searching for this one. They must have found her dead friends by now."

"Really? It's a *her* now? That's how this plays out?" Rogers grunted, the hours of movement without resting taking a toll on him. "You never stop, do you?"

"Don't get all excited, even a boar hog can be a she; it doesn't mean I'm going to go exchanging phone numbers and asking her to prom."

Rogers shook his head in frustration and moved back against a bench. "If you're serious, then have at it. Get the clothes off this thing," he said, leaning back in surrender.

Jacob sat up. "Why don't you just ask it first?"

James turned and looked back at him. "Ask?"

"She knows we'll find out anyhow. I'm sure she's been listening—"

Rogers sighed and shook his head. "And now here you go with the *she*."

Jacob ignored the comment and continued. "This is a good test; give it up the easy way or we find it the hard way. Let's see what she has to say. We need to know what's going on out there."

James shrugged, looking over to Rogers. "He's got a point; why take her alive if we weren't planning to use her for something?" The leader returned an apathetic shrug in response.

James inched closer to the restrained alien. The creature had not moved since it was dropped to the floor hours earlier. Men along the walls, sensing something was about to happen, adjusted their posture, their full attention now focused on the creature.

James grabbed at the alien's uniform and yanked it into an upright, seated position, forcing its head away from him. He worked on the knot of fabric at the base of its neck and tugged the satchel from its face.

The alien squinted in the light; its bright blue eyes closed tightly and slowly opened. Jacob saw sadness in the creature's face. He began to feel pangs of sympathy before he caught himself, remembering what this thing was capable of. He looked around the room and could see the other soldiers were having the same reaction. James reached ahead and pulled away a final strip of fabric that had bound its mouth. Once its lips were free, it swiveled its head smoothly, examining the room and the faces of the strange men.

"Why have you taken me? Where am I?" she asked in a soft voice.

Jacob was amazed that the tone was matter of fact, the English clean and crisp. She showed no signs of fear or displays of emotion. The creature sounded unconcerned, even though its eyes deceived it.

"This is my summer guest house. I want to apologize in advance; the lake house is being renovated, and the housekeeper is home with a sick kid," James said.

"Guest house?" she asked, puzzled.

Rogers shook his head, not amused. "Just ask."

James frowned. Using his thumb and index finger, he stroked the heavy beard covering his chin. "Are you wearing a locator?"

Without answering, she gave him a puzzled expression.

"Are you wearing anything that will allow your people to find you?" he said, speaking slow and deliberately.

"Why would I have such a device? No member of the communal is any more valuable than another."

"So where is it? How do they track you?" James asked.

She looked at him absently. "Why would they track me?"

James cracked his knuckles, letting his eyes examine her uniform, looking for anything distinct. "Well … since you say there is no device, I guess we can cut all of your clothing off and shred it. According to you, I will find nothing and that would prove you are truthful." He stared at the alien and saw her expression hadn't changed. "*Or*, we search your clothing and find a device. Then—well, let's just say it'd be better if I found you trustworthy, and you just gave it to me *now*."

"I don't understand your reasoning," she said.

James reached to his hip and drew a long, custom Ka-Bar.

"I'm just saying it isn't healthy to be caught in a lie. You sure you ain't got something on you?"

He leaned in close, slowly turning the blade so the alien could see it from every angle while the light reflected off the sharpened surface. James grabbed the chest of her uniform with his gloved hand and pulled it tight. "Now you'll have to take it easy on me. I'm not used to undressing ladies this way." She drew away from him. He stuck the blade close to the fabric and let the razor-sharp knife sink into the material. It cut as easy as silk, quickly splitting with slow movements of the blade.

She lugged back again and turned her head to the side. "Yes, I have such a device."

"Ah, really? You mind telling me where it is?"

She stretched out her bound arms and looked to her balled up left hand. "It's in the glove."

Rogers stood from the bench he was leaning on. "Now hold up; that's the weaponized hand." He moved forward so he was in front of her. "Tell us how to safely remove it, or I'll cut the entire arm off."

She scowled, turning away from Rogers, not liking his harsh tones. "The glove cannot be removed with my hand like this."

Losing patience, Jesse stood up and, moving closer, he said, "Let's just kill this thing and get rid of it." He stepped close to get a better view. Other men nodded, agreeing with him.

She shook her head, worry now clearly showing in her eyes. "The glove is not a weapon. It is not lethal. Only designed to render obedience."

"I can think of only one good way to do this." Rogers reached out violently and grabbed her bound wrists, pulling them tight, and dragging the alien partway across the floor as she whined in protest. Then he brought in his boot and stepped on her forearms, applying so much pressure that Jacob thought her arms might break. She yelped and cried out in pain, having been surprised by the big man's sudden movements.

"What the hell are you doing?" James said. "Take it easy, boss."

Rogers turned his head. "Shut up and get it off. Cut it at the elbow."

"No … take it easy. Let me try first. I can get it off. " James scrambled, grabbing at the thing's fingertips. The alien, frightened yet complying, straightened them just enough so that James could slowly roll the glove off of the creature's hands. All the while, the thing struggled and kicked against Rogers's boot.

"I got it," James said, pulling back at the strips of heavy tape before taking the metallic glove tight in his hand.

Rogers stepped away and the alien pulled back, crashing against the wall and bringing its hands up to shield its now tear-covered face.

"Well, look at that … the space lady has feelings," Rogers said, unaffected.

Jesse stepped closer, pointing at the alien's face. "Don't let it fool you, Sarge; it's a killer. I saw them firsthand."

"You are the killers," she gasped.

Ignoring her comment, James laughed as he stretched the glove out and examined it. "Relax guys, we got it off," he said.

He turned the glove over; in the palm was a diamond-shaped pendant. All the fingers were coated in a type of silicone with embedded circuitry clearly visible. James stretched the glove out and laid it flat on his palm, the entire piece far smaller than his own hand.

"What does it do?"

"It's of no use to you," she said.

James grinned and let out a short laugh. "That's not what I asked. So this is what you used to knock me on my ass; how is it powered?"

"I don't understand."

Jacob scooched closer; he reached out for the glove and James obliged by handing it over. He felt the wires and squeezed the pendant between his fingers. "The energy source; what activates the crystal?"

"It is part of my being; the same as how the rifles are part of the Ursus warriors. We all have a role."

James took the glove back. "Ursus? You mean the big bastards with the red sleeves?"

"I understand your word *bastard*, and this is not correct. The Ursus are brave warriors, bred for war; they come from strong family units."

James smiled and glanced at the pant legs of his uniform, where he'd wiped his hands earlier. "Well, they bleed like pigs." James looked her in the eye and saw he got no response from his comment. "How many Ursus will they send for you?" he asked.

She eyed up at him. "I'm not important enough for them to look for me."

"Who are you?"

"I am Karina, a guide for my people."

"What were you doing out here?"

"I am a guide; I was searching for survivors so that they could be safely returned to the community."

"You mean prisoners." Jacob leaned in. "What have you done with them?"

She shot him a puzzled glance. “We have cared for them, given them food and shelter; they are part of the communal now.”

“You have my family; I want them back.”

“Then you should join them. All are welcome in the communal.”

Answering for Jacob, James scoffed. “My people got a saying, lady … better dead than red!”

She pursed her lips. “I don’t understand this *red*.”

Rogers laughed and said, “Different time, but the same principle applies. We’ll get our people back.”

James nodded and winked at her. “We need a vehicle to get into that camp,” he said before he turned to Rogers still standing over his shoulder. “How many claymore mines do we have left?”

Rogers smiled, knowing the bearded scout’s intentions. “We can spare a couple.”

She glared up at him. “Why would you need mines?”

“I figured we could see if you’re right—that they wouldn’t bother looking for you. I’ll stack the dead out there and this glove right down the throat of a mine."

Her eyes shifted from the glove and back to the door. "There is no more cause for this violence; if you lay down your weapons it could all stop."

"Nope. That's not our way," Rogers said. "Thought we explained that."

"You must understand … the war is over. You have lost."

James shook his head. "I think you're the one who is not understanding. You all just got here; we weren't even trying earlier."

"Your big cities have already fallen, and your armies destroyed or surrendered. Only small pockets of resistance remain, and they will be squashed with the exodus." Her tone changed from weakness to one of strength.

Rogers stepped over her and looked down. "Bullshit. What is the exodus?"

She smiled, showing perfectly shaped white teeth. "Our people will arrive. What you have seen is only an advanced party meaning to pull out and detect your remaining forces. The exodus will force you to submit and join us or cease to exist."

"Why the hell would you tell us this, anyway?" James said arrogantly.

"It is our law. You have captured me rightfully in combat or by submission; I now belong to you," she said. "Same as your people now in the communal belong to us."

"Unless we take them back," Jacob retorted.

She nodded in agreement. "Yes, of course. Or if you surrender and become a part of us."

"You'd be surprised what it takes for us to surrender," James spat back.

Karina openly smiled at his statement. "Surprisingly little; your governments have already petitioned for peace. Your people have been approaching our communities of their own free will offering surrender, and once others hear the peace signal, we expect your remaining forces to join the communal."

Jacob reached out and put a hand on Rogers's shoulder. "The people at the orb … the civilians … the ones being escorted by The Darkness—"

"Escorted for their protection," Karina interrupted. "Tribes and those like you have become a danger to everyone. If you had not fired on our landers …"

Rogers put up a hand between Jacob and the alien. "You said peace signal?"

She nodded, taking her eyes from Jacob's hateful stare. "Yes, it is being broadcast now, over clear channels, on what you call FM."

Rogers scrambled to the back, pushing the soldier away from the radio console. "We've only been searching our military frequencies; of course we should have looked at the local FM." He flipped dials and switched a speaker, filling the space with static. He dialed the knob until it locked on a clear, clean channel with a steady voice.

"... lay down your weapons, the armed resistance has been disbanded. We have lost our ability to fight back. For the sake of all of us, I ask that you surrender and go to the road un-armed. You will be given sanctuary; food and shelter will be provided. Our friends have guaranteed our safety. Please ... this is the only way to stop the bloodshed."

Jacob thought he recognized the voice and whispered, "He sounds familiar."

“It’s the Vice President,” a soldier in the back uttered. “What does this mean?”

Rogers flipped off the radio. “Don’t mean nothing; we go in tomorrow.”

Chapter 25

They stood two deep, partially concealed in the tree lines and overgrown grass. Sunlight reflected off the blued barrels of their rifles. The Darkness had them surrounded, but for some reason still hadn't moved against them.

Clem stood on a wooden crate, observing them through a hole in the brick wall of the warehouse while the survivors had moved to the rear of the large building. The space, which looked like a loading dock, was filled with vehicles of all make and model and had two tall overhead doors chained shut at the end of the wall. The women ran about, hurriedly packing their gear and preparing for a hasty withdrawal.

"How many?" Masterson asked. Standing just below Clem, the old soldier was pulling belts of linked ammo from his pack and prepping his machine gun for a fight.

"Got to be over a hundred of 'em."

"And the uniformed critters?" Masterson asked.

Clem shook his head then leapt off the crate. "None yet."

Ruth rushed up behind them, followed by a group of girls carrying large duffel bags and boxes of canned goods. She stopped beside them as the other girls continued to load the vehicles. "We're going to break out," she said. "If we hurry, we can make the woods before they organize. If their vehicles show up, we won't have a chance."

Clem watched as children were loaded into the cabs of vans and pickup trucks parked in long columns just behind the sliding doors of the warehouse. Women with worried expressions stood watch over the vehicles as the precious cargo was loaded.

"No, it won't work," Clem said, not taking his eyes from the vehicles.

"What choice do we have? We can't stand against this many; they'll have us completely blocked in soon enough."

Clem looked down, locking eyes with Masterson, who nodded in response. "Get us someplace high; we'll help you get past them. If you have any of those Molotovs left, we could use them."

Ruth gazed at them and then back to the overloaded vehicles. "You don't have to do this. We'd have a chance on the road."

Clem shrugged. "Like you said, what choice do you have? We can cover you and fight it out on our own. Just get your people someplace safe."

Ruth frowned and pointed to a wooden crate along the wall. "There … that's what we have left. At the end of the room you'll find an iron staircase; it leads to the roof." She stepped forward and grabbed Clem in a tight-gripped bear hug. "We can't thank you enough for this," she whispered to him.

"Just wait for us to open fire then get them out of here. Get as far away from this place as you can," Clem said.

She let go and gave Masterson the same kind of hug before turning away and barking orders at the girls, rushing them to finish loading. Clem watched her leave before looking over at his friend. "You ready to go to work?"

Masterson dipped his chin and lifted the heavy machine gun to his chest. "Yeah, too much estrogen in this place. Let's get up top. I need some fresh air."

Moving past him, Clem slapped his friend on the shoulder. They stopped at the crate, grabbing as many bottles as they could carry, before moving to the staircase. The stairs were old and screeched as they climbed them. The spots where wrought iron brackets met the brick shook and spit crumbled mortar in protest. The stairway ended at a pigeon-feces-covered exit. Clem passed through the doorway and stepped onto the roof. The perimeter of the area was lined with a three-foot-tall, red brick knee wall. In the middle, surrounded by rotting piles of leaves, empty trash cans, and liquor bottles probably left by exploring teens, stood the remains of a crumbled utility building.

Clem heard the truck engines fire up below and knew they were ready. He pointed to a section of the low wall that would be to the right of the overhead doors below. "You post up there; I'll take the other side."

Masterson nodded and dropped down, duck-walking to sneak into cover without the Deltas on the ground spotting them. Clem did the same by belly crawling up to the knee wall and letting the barrel of his rifle slowly move into position. He looked across the opening to Masterson and waited for the man to flash him a thumbs up before he crept his head over the ledge.

All along the front the things waited. Still standing shoulder to shoulder in some sort of wall, it would make for easy shooting. From the overhead door, a cracked and broken asphalt drive wended away before vanishing into the thick of the woods, giving the trucks a reasonable chance of escape. When he heard the engines revving below, Clem searched for targets, trying to identify a leader or an obvious choice to kick off the attack. Out of the corner of his eye, he spotted a cluster of the Deltas charging forward. He'd waited too long, maybe it was too late.

Masterson also saw the rushing group; without hesitation, he lit the first of his Molotovs and tossed it into the open ground just in front of the advancing group. With the splash of flame, the remaining Deltas began to scream.

A round whizzed over Clem's head while another struck the brick wall to his front. With no need for instructions, he pulled the rifle into his shoulder and began firing on targets, picking those with automatic weapons first.

Masterson's machine gun let loose at the same time as the overhead doors began screeching open. The first of the trucks racing forward, Masterson changed the angle of his fire just enough to allow the vehicles to move through the wall of lead he was providing.

The convoy was taking heavy fire. Clem laid down his rifle and rolled to his side, lighting the fire bombs and tossing them in rapid succession to his left and right, trying to create a gauntlet of flames for the vehicles to race down.

Clem watched in horror as the Deltas on the ground began ignoring them. Instead, The Darkness focused all of their fire on the escaping vehicles. A gray cargo van took heavy fire, rounds drumming across its front. Clem figured the driver must have been killed as he watched the van veer hard, nearly rolling before sliding partially off the asphalt and colliding with a tree just short of the opening to the road. Vehicles behind it slammed to a stop, while some tried to steer right of the disabled van, the back half of it now blocking the road.

A wave of at least ten Deltas emerged from the trees, screaming as they charged forward at the van. Clem went back to the weapon, his bolt-action rifle not able to keep up with the mobs. The things reached the van door and began grabbing at the woman and children inside. He no longer had a safe shot and was forced to get off target. He switched his aim in an attempt to support the other vehicles and watched as women exited with weapons in hand, fighting bravely while trying to cover the others as they escaped.

Masterson stayed on the machine gun, screaming as he fired, bringing his aim in as close to the women on the ground as he safely could. "Oh my god, here they come!" he shouted. Clem gaped down and saw the first of the red-sleeved soldiers appear in the tree line, their vehicles just becoming visible in the distant trees. The Deltas were handing off their captives to them. Looking down, Clem could see some of the armed women were falling to the heavy fire, while others were retreating back to the warehouse. He clenched his teeth and looked away from the carnage below, instead focusing on the red-sleeved soldiers standing to his front.

Clem's guts ached and his throat constricted as he realized they'd failed. This was a fight he knew he couldn't win. He pushed away the dread and steadied his aim, firing a shot directly into a creature's chest. He worked the bolt, loading another .308 round and took down another creature before the first had even fallen. A blue splash of plasma erupted to his right, and he felt the heat on his cheek. Ignoring the pain, he reloaded and dropped another of the alien soldiers.

"Clem, we need to move!" Masterson yelled.

He loaded another round and panned left. Having dropped the first group of alien soldiers, he searched the tree line for more. An enemy squad was kneeling in the trees. He locked onto one and saw he was looking down the barrel of an enemy rifle … they fired at the same time. He watched the soldier's helmeted head snap back from his round as the bolt of blue plasma raced in his direction. With a yank at his boot, Clem was jerked away. He felt himself being dragged across the roof just as the knee wall to his front exploded.

He rolled to his back and looked into the tired face of Masterson. "I said we have to move! There's nothing else we can do here," his friend yelled.

"No, I won't leave!" Clem protested over the sounds of screaming children below. He tried to roll back to his belly and return to the wall. He knew the fight was over, that the Deltas were taking them all away, but he would do whatever he could to stop it.

Masterson low-crawled to his side and, pushing his face in close, said, "We can't help them if we're dead."

Clem acknowledged him with a slow nod, biting into his bottom lip until it bled.

He watched as Masterson searched the roof. The building itself was engulfed in flames, and black smoke was pouring up the stairway they'd used earlier.

"There," Masterson said, pointing to the back corner of the building, which appeared to be the only place flames weren't licking over the sides of the roof.

On their stomachs, they crawled together. As they neared the back of the building, the incoming fire stopped and the screams faded into the distance; only the sounds of the roaring fire remained. They moved along in a drainage trench that followed the edge of the roof, finding a hole cut in the side that allowed rainwater to drain from the flat roof. Looking over the edge of the knee wall, they could see what remained of an ancient, tin downspout.

Masterson reached over and nudged it with his boot. He rose up and looked back at Clem. "Looks solid enough. I'll go first." The man dropped over the side and disappeared. Not wanting to be left alone, Clem scrambled after him, nearly falling as he grasped the pipe and slid to the ground. He landed hard, feeling his old knees crunch from the speed of the drop. He turned away and pressed his back to the wall while flames and smoke rolled from windows overhead.

Masterson turned an eye back at him. "You okay, old timer?"

Clem flipped him a middle finger. "Lead us out," he said.

Masterson scaled ahead slowly, patrolling them along the perimeter of the building, rounding the corner, and coming into view of the far side to the place where the vehicles had attempted to flee from.

The enemy was gone; the ground littered with their dead.

Looking toward the blacktop road, Clem stared mesmerized at the burning hulks of the vans and pickup trucks once filled with children. He staggered closer, stopping at the body of a woman he didn't recognize. He knelt beside her and used his palm to close her eyes.

"Over here," Masterson said from farther ahead and closer to the building.

In a depression lay the body of Grandmother; the red-haired woman's chest was covered in blood and she was wheezing. Masterson pulled her from the ditch and rested her head on his lap. He put a hand to her bloody chest then looked up at Clem, shaking his head. She strained to move and pointed at her pack. "Get it for me," she gasped.

Clem moved to the spot and retrieved a small bag and placed it by her side. She fumbled through a front pouch and fished out the small notebook. She pushed it in Clem's direction as she coughed and blood curled over her bottom lip. "Get my girls back," she whispered.

She reached a hand back and Masterson took it. He felt her grasp loosen as the old woman wheezed and drew her last breaths. Slowly and gently, he rolled her head from his lap. "What are we going to do?" he said, examining the destruction surrounded in the flames of the burning vehicles and warehouse.

Clem lowered his head and sucked in a deep breath before dropping to his knees. Falling back on his rear, he flipped through pages of the notebook, stopping at a hand-drawn map of a small, walled village with an orb positioned in the center. "I'm going to get them back, or kill as many of those things as I can trying," he said.

Chapter 26

She stood by the picture window, watching as new arrivals were marched down the center of the street. Unlike the last ones, some men were present in this group. Ragged and in torn clothing, they were under close guard as they carried suitcases and held the hands of children. Rows of the armed black-eyed Deltas and several of the red-sleeved soldiers were always close by, unlike other groups of new arrivals.

The people were being herded toward wide, blue, steel transports. A group of guides stood near the transports, examining each person before directing them to the back of a cargo hold. Watching, Laura was able to detect a pattern; the young and healthy always moved to the left, while the old and sick to the right. She turned and looked to Francis who was sitting at the dining room table, eating a small meal of cheese and sliced meats—the man was spending more time at the house now.

They'd barely spoken since she'd returned from the kitchen duty. Out of fear that her words may be true, she didn't want to bring up her conversation with the old woman—that Francis was now her mate. She shook her head, refusing to accept the idea. Instead, she asked, "What are they doing with them?"

Francis kept his eyes on the plate to his front. "The local population is being relocated; well … those sensible enough to join us."

She glanced back at the transports then to Francis. "Why separate them?"

Francis lifted a fork-full of meat to his mouth and chewed slowly. He turned and looked Laura in the eyes then waved a hand at her dismissively. "Because of your people's refusal to surrender, resources are now scarce; we don't have enough for everyone. They have destroyed too much of our infrastructure and transports, as well as our ability to gather more. Because of their ignorance, this place is no longer safe for us."

"What does that mean?"

"It means choices have to be made, not all will be allowed to move with us."

With her breath held to control her emotions, she turned and approached the table. "What do you mean *move*?" Laura asked.

“The council has decided to give up on this area; we will be leaving soon.”

She took a pitcher of water from the table and refilled his drinking glass. Francis looked up and acknowledged her actions with a smile. “Leaving?” she asked.

He nodded, lifting the glass and taking a long drink. “We will join the large communities in the city. This communal will be abandoned. They never should have attempted to settle here so far from support in the first place. Once we leave, the surrounding areas will be quelled by the witnesses. Maybe we can return one day when it’s safe.”

“Quelled?” Laura said, unable to hide the horror in her voice.

“Yes, it will take time, but they will bring this place to peace,” Francis said calmly.

“By killing everything?”

Francis swore under his breath before looking up at her. “It is unfortunate, but the local population refuses to submit. What other choice do they have? The people committing these crimes have to be dealt with.”

Laura returned to the window and pulled back the curtain, pointing to the right trailer. She turned back and began shaking her head at the man. "And what of them? You didn't explain why they are separating them."

Francis snorted and laid his fork beside his plate. "Those not chosen to continue on our path will be given the gift of the message. They will become witness to the truth and continue our fight here."

She shook her head and backed away from the window, watching as an old man pushed a boy in a wheelchair up the ramp of a transport to the right. "You've lied to them all; they think you will protect them."

"And we are protecting them. Those people are old and sick; when they awaken, they will be strong and a vibrant part of the communal."

"They need to be warned." She turned from the window and rushed to the door. Francis got there first and blocked her with his shoulder. Knocking her away, she fell hard to the floor. He stepped close to her, and reached down, offering her a hand. She slapped it away.

"We leave tonight," he said, returning to the table. "Ready the child."

Laura tried to steady herself to push back her anger. "I won't leave; not without my husband," she scowled.

Francis smiled at her, already knowing that she'd learned the truth of their relationship. "Your old life is behind you. I am your husband now. Gather your things and ready the child."

She scrambled to her feet and backed away from him, almost falling against the dinner table. "We won't leave with you. We won't go anywhere with you."

He stood and squared his chest to her. He pushed forward, the softness gone in his voice. His face was hard and intimidating. "You don't have a choice. The war is over; we've won. Your governments—your people—have surrendered to *us*!"

She stepped back, bumping the table and knocking over the drinking glass and pitcher. Laura fumbled, steadying herself, and her hand brushed the side of the heavy clay pitcher. She quickly reached out and took it. Then, swinging hard, she smashed it against Francis's head. The man stumbled back, surprised, putting a hand to his bloodied face. He lunged at her. She dodged and ran for the hallway, sprinting to Katy's room. She made it just ahead of him, slamming the door, and leaving him to pound against it.

She felt the pressure cease against the door then heard the clunk of a bolt lock. She stood and backed away. Katy was sitting on the floor looking up at her with wide eyes. She moved back and fell to the carpet beside her daughter. She raised the girl onto her lap, and Katy gripped her hands. "Are you scared, Momma?"

Laura nodded, trying to hold back the tears. "We have to leave now; we have to escape."

She grabbed Katy and stood her up. Finding her coat and long pants, she dressed her in heavy clothing then put boots on her feet. She felt the tears falling on her cheeks as she reached out and took her daughter again, holding the girl tight to her chest. "What have I done …?" she said.

"It's okay, Daddy will come back."

Laura nodded, forcing a smile. "We're gonna find him; we'll leave tonight." She snatched a rat tail comb from the dresser and pulled the girl's hair back, tying it up, then put a heavy hat over her head. All of her own clothing was in the other room; she would have to leave with what she had on. She wasn't dressed for the cold, but she would take her chances.

Prepared to move to the only bedroom window, she heard a knock at the door. The bolt turned and released. Laura stood and pushed Katy behind her. Taking the rat tail comb in her hand, she concealed it behind her back.

"Mrs. Anderson," a familiar voice called as a woman in dark robes entered the room.

"Taurine!" Laura said, surprised to see the old woman. "What are you doing here?"

"Your mate sent for me. He is afraid for you; afraid for your daughter." Taurine strained and saw Katy dressed for travel. Her gaze traveled up and met Laura's.

"Were you planning on going somewhere? Do you know what will happen to you if he reports this?"

Laura shook her head and leered down. "Is that why you're here? Are you going to take me away?"

Taurine smiled and stepped closer. "No, silly woman; I am here to discipline you, to teach you to be more respectful of your husband."

Laura watched as the old woman slipped the small metal box from her pocket. She felt the knowledge plate on the top of her head begin to tingle.

"Don't worry. As I promised your husband, this lesson will be discreet. I've come alone; this will be just between us. If the others knew, they would reject you."

Laura backed away as the woman stepped closer. Taurine rubbed a finger along the top of the box and the tingling on Laura's head buzzed with intensity, pain beginning to form in the back of her skull. Taurine stepped closer, now within arm's reach.

"We have much to discuss, Mrs. Anderson. I knew from the moment I met you, that you would be difficult."

She raised the box so it was at Laura's eye level. "I'm sorry, but you have to learn the price for disobedience," Taurine said, slowly sliding her thumb down the box.

Laura felt weakness in her legs. The woman was now so close Laura could see the pores on her skin. Suddenly Laura no longer felt afraid, the fear replaced by anger. She no longer hesitated; she feigned turning away to the left, while lashing out with the rat tail comb gripped tightly in her right hand. The tip of the spear caught Taurine just below the jugular. The old woman screamed and dove at Laura, her hand clasping the metal box tight. Laura felt shooting pain in her head and her vision filled with bolts of blinding light.

She fought through the agony to maintain the grip on the comb as she forced it deeper into Taurine's neck, twisting it as it burrowed its way to her spinal cord. When the plastic tip broke, Laura punched at the wound and the side of the woman's head. Taurine screamed something as her hot blood poured down Laura's arm. The old woman gagged, spitting blood; her grip relaxed and Laura felt the relief and release of the knowledge plate.

Her vision returned to her in the scene of a nightmare, the old woman's blood covering her body. She wanted to scream, but she saw Katy standing against the wall, her face white with shock. Laura pushed the old woman off of her and rolled back to her knees, pushing herself up to her feet. She looked at the door and wondered if Francis was in the house. Maybe she could sneak past him.

She gripped Katy's hand and led her from the room, locking the door behind her. She stalked down the hallway and found the home empty, the front door unlocked. Quickly, she moved to the back of the house where the kitchen door led into the backyard. This door was bolted, but could be opened without a key; she quickly unlocked it and looked out into a fenced-in yard. She knelt down next to Katy and whispered, "We have to go now; you have to be very quiet, okay?"

Katy nodded. "We're going to find Daddy."

"That's right, Katy. We're going to find Daddy."

Chapter 27

They hid in a small cluster of homes just off the main road and prepared the ambush behind a series of parallel parked cars. The homes around them were destroyed, doors removed and windows shattered, leaving no doubt as to why the owners had abandoned this area or been forcibly removed. Two red-sleeved bodies lay dead in the center of the street while the gold glove was placed over one of the car's radio antennas in a mock salute.

The Assassins had placed four claymore mines in a circle, all of them pointed in. The intent was to lead the enemy into the kill zone then blow the directional mines. There was no discussion over ethics or further attacks while the VP was calling for a surrender. They were all in agreement that they would continue the fight as long as they had the means. And today that meant taking the fight directly to them. Jacob felt the tickle in his ear, predicting the oncoming vehicles. He lowered himself behind a windowsill of a house directly across from the ambush kill box—he would have a front-seat view.

Jesse was next to him, once again carrying a heavy machine gun; he sat with his back to the wall and the weapon rested on his lap. Karina was bound and restrained in the kitchen of the home. Several walls were missing, exposing blackened and charred framing and allowing the men to see from one end of the house to the other.

Jacob turned back and caught a glimpse of one of their more injured soldiers. Refusing to stay behind, the man was now on guard duty, standing watch over the alien prisoner. Even though she had given allegiance to them and agreed to full cooperation, calling it their way, Karina hadn't come close to earning their trust. Jacob turned back to the front and strained to find the rest of the group. He knew they were scattered among the remaining homes, waiting for the approaching enemy and the blast of the mines that would trigger the ambush.

Moving at them from the east, the road traveled through the cluster of homes and sloped down a hill, the top covered in the fog of early morning. The heavy mist blanketed the ground, and the sun rising behind the hilltop made it difficult to see through. Jacob watched intently as the first of the red-sleeved soldiers appeared, emerging from the cloud like a hazy ghost. They were walking in a triangle formation. Rifles at the low ready, they were scouting the way for a column of three vehicles that gradually materialized behind them, the hovercrafts' engines blowing and dispersing the light fog surrounding them.

The approaching soldiers paused and seemed to signal, pointing at the waiting bait pile. A Red aimed his rifle toward the suspended golden glove and the Reds approached it, the vehicles moving in closer to provide security. The three-soldier patrol stopped at the first of the destroyed cars and allowed one of the hovercrafts to pass by. The vehicle sped past the glove and stopped just shy of leaving the kill zone. Jacob knew from its angle that it had parked almost directly in front of one of the claymore mines. The next two vehicles raced ahead, moving into position and creating a triangular formation nearly identical to the one the Reds had been walking.

The hovercrafts were being cautious, parking tactically and using dismounts for support in an attempt to shield themselves from danger. Ironically, their parking spots put them in the sights of a cauldron of mines. *They have a lot to learn about the human style of warfare,* Jacob thought.

He was ready to rise up over the window sill and take aim when Jesse grabbed his elbow. “Wait,” the big man whispered.

With a clanging of gears, the hovercrafts anchored and ramps began to drop. Groups of soldiers and Golds exited through the rear of the transports.

Knowing what was about to happen, Jacob winced, almost allowing pity to enter his mind. They had never intended to do this much damage. Now, with nearly twenty-five of the creatures—several unarmed—loitering in the kill box, he second-guessed the plan. *Maybe this is too much*, he thought. He then remembered the strike against Meaford and the devastation of the Deltas on his hometown of Chicago. *No ... this was just enough.*

Reds spread out and posted up security, having no idea they were looking down the face of a mine and about to receive a dose of 700 steel ball bearings propelled by high explosives. Other groups of soldiers formed working parties, recovering the dead bodies and returning them to one of the vehicles. The Reds were lax and at ease, still feeling they were the APEX predator in the area. A pack of Golds approached the suspended glove and pointed at it suspiciously.

"What is he waiting for?" Jacob whispered.

A Gold moved closer and extended a hand to the antenna; it grabbed the golden glove and began to remove it from the wire. Knowing it was about to happen, Jacob squeezed his rifle's stock. The view to his front vanished in a flash of lightning, fire, and black smoke. The ground lifted and crashed under his feet; the house rattled and cracked from the shock waves of the explosives and stray fragments of the mines. Jacob leaned forward out of the window with Jesse by his side, searching for targets. Every alien was down, and two of the three vehicles were engulfed in metallic flame.

He stood and bounded over the windowsill. Approaching the kill box, he saw grotesquely maimed bodies spread out on the ground. A Red struggling to rise caught his attention; Jacob raised his rifle and put quick shots into its body. Just then, a blue flash raced by him and he spotted a small squad of dazed and scattered Reds—somehow spared the carnage of the mines—slowly recovering and firing blind. He crouched for cover between the cars as Jesse leveled his machine gun and let loose several long bursts, shredding their bodies.

More gun shots sounded from the opposite side of the ambush; Jacob knew it would be Rogers and his own team moving in. Jacob crouched and shuffle stepped forward, his rifle up while he surveyed the damage. Slowly he stepped into the spoiled ground of the ambush site. The alien bodies at his feet were mangled and twisted, still smoldering from the mine. The car where the golden glove had been was now folded and crumpled, all of its windows gone, and a tattering of Gold bodies lay strewn beside it. Jacob saw the remnants of the glove near the bloody pulp of an alien body. He reached down and held it up, showing it to Jesse.

"Hold on to it, maybe it'll bring us good luck," Jesse said.

Jacob stuffed the glove into a breast pocket and stood his ground, watching while Rogers came into view from the far side the remaining vehicle. The leader had his hand up, pointing out positions and directing other soldiers into security zones. He looked at Jacob then put two fingers to his eyes and pointed at the remaining vehicle, the only one not burning. They merged on it from opposite angles, walking in arcs so that their rifles were aimed into the rear compartment. The back crew space was empty. With a steel box and bench seats along the bulkheads, it didn't appear to be any different from human transportation.

The front is where things changed. An empty driver's seat sat in the center, surrounded by flat-panel consoles and operators' chairs, also empty. There were sparks and smoke coming from some of the stations, but the vehicle still floated at an anchored hover and appeared stable. Rogers looked to a soldier behind him. "Go fetch me our alien," he ordered.

The soldier gave a quick nod and turned to run away.

Jacob shadowed Rogers as he moved deeper into the compartment, examining the cold metallic surfaces and the monitors filled with foreign text and flickering images. Most of the seats were small and compact, apparently built around the small frames of the guides. "What do you make of this?" he asked.

Rogers stepped closer and observed the bench seats, running his hands over the plush fabric and looking down at golden uniform items left behind. "This isn't a combat vehicle; looks like some kind of mobile command center or intel truck. Probably why the Gold fucks were in it."

"Sergeant," the soldier called from behind. He and another soldier had Karina locked in a grip between them. Her face was distraught and sickly from having just waded through the bodies of her own dead.

She turned to Rogers. "Why have you done this? Why must you continue this senseless fight?"

"This is war, sweetheart," James said, pushing up beside her. "Just be happy you're on our side now." He grasped her by the elbow, taking her from the escorting soldiers, and led her deeper into the crew compartment then dropped her into a seat behind one of the consoles.

Rogers moved so that he stood over her. "You say you'll help us? It's time to put up or shut up."

She looked up at him. "I'm not sure what you expect me to do."

"I want to know what's going on in that walled city."

She nodded her head and moved her hands to a graphite black bar. Before her hands took hold of it, Rogers grabbed her wrist. "No tricks," he said sternly.

She swallowed hard and continued her hand to the bar. "This is a musing transport. It is not designed for battle. Guides, like myself, use it for meditation, to gather information, and to interpret findings. You should not have killed these people; they wouldn't have fought you."

"Spilt milk," Rogers said. "You might say your Goldies are friendly, but those other guys sure as hell aren't."

Karina scowled, glaring down in disgust before looking up at him. "My people are no friend to the Ursus."

James laughed, moving closer and plopping onto an alien bench. "Oh, so now it's *my people,* and *hey, look at me, I hate them just as much as you do.* Bullshit, you are happy as a pig in shit back in your little hippie commune and now you want to feed us your sad story."

She shook her head before powering up the console, moving her hands along the graphite bar. "Before Earth, the Ursus captured my home world. There is no human word to describe my people; we were given the gift of the message a millennium ago. The Ursus came to enforce the message." She paused, looking away. "The Ursus are not of my race, even though we now all share a common creator."

"Their creator is Ursus?" Jacob asked.

"No, the *Creator* is the *creator*; the Ursus are just another member of our communal. We all serve a purpose under the eyes of the Creator—the Ursus are warriors; we are spiritual and technical minded."

James shrugged, leaning back and calling Duke up to his lap. "Well, I say kill 'em all and let God sort 'em out. And just to avoid any confusion, I'm talking about my God, not your hocus pocus man behind the curtain gibberish."

Rogers grunted. "Enough. Karina … what can you tell me about their base?"

Her hand moved along the bar, the display changing light patterns as it scrolled from left to right in bouncing waves of green and blue. She was unable to hide a shocked expression and pulled her hand back as if it were on fire.

"What did you see?" Jacob asked her.

She turned and looked him in the eye. "We can't stay here. We need to get very far away."

"Why? What's happening?"

"They have initiated a dissolution protocol for this region. The Council has lost patience with the death of our ... *their* Messenger."

Rogers pointed at her. "Cut the bullshit. What does this mean in human?"

"They will leave and take the community with them."

Jacob pushed forward. "No ... we have to stop them."

"That isn't all," Karina said in a lower tone. "They will release the wit—" She stopped, thinking of the human word. "They will release the Deltas on this area. Not only that, they will rapidly multiply the number of them. This region will be blocked off until nothing living remains. My people call this 'the quell'."

Rogers clenched his fist, looking at her then catching the fear in Jacob's eyes. "When is this going to happen?"

"It's already begun," she said. "This patrol was out looking for survivors and recovering the dead; the last mission before the area is abandoned and moved to the south."

Rogers turned and called to the pair of soldiers waiting at the bottom of the ramp. He removed a dog-eared notebook from his chest pocket and wrote a series of instructions then folded the paper and placed it into the palm of the nearest soldier. "I need you to get back to the tower and get on the radio, the same frequency they are using. The tower should have the power to override their transmission. I want you to call out to anyone and everyone in the area to converge on the community. The grid coordinates are on the paper. We have to attack and destroy it now, or everyone in this area will be killed."

"Wait, I can do better," Karina said. "This vehicle has the ability to change and rebroadcast the message. The community will not know that it's happening."

Rogers looked at her. "Why would you do that?"

"I told you … I am now one of you; I belong to your communal. It is our way."

"Then get it done. Do it now," Rogers said.

He turned back to the soldier. "I need you to get back to Meaford. According to our turncoat here, the area should be clear. You need to rally everyone and get them moving against the orb. We need to attack at dusk. Do you understand?"

"Yes, Sergeant."

"Move … we're counting on you," Rogers said. He paused and turned to Karina. "Can you drive this hippie wagon?"

Chapter 28

Laura stumbled into the darkness of the backyard. There were no lights, only the moonlight reflecting off the high steel wall circling the communal. She moved along a clapboard fence, pulling Katy behind her and searching for a place to hide. She knew Francis would return soon and she needed to be gone. When he found Taurine, he would report her, then the Deltas would come. She crept along the fence, wending her way through an overgrown garden, deeper into high grass and away from the homes along the street.

The tall and solid wall reflected back at her mockingly; she wouldn't be able to escape this way. A noise in the house startled her. Someone was pounding on the locked door—they would find Taurine soon. She needed someplace to hide, to get as far from here as she could. She pressed against the clapboard fence, searching the boards. She found loose panels and pried at them with her bare hands, scraping her knuckles until they bled. A board came loose. She pulled it free and worked on the one next to it, finding it easier to pull away.

Laura stuck her head through the hole in the fence, searching until she was sure the way was clear. Quickly, she whirled back and guided Katy through the opening ahead of her. She scrambled through just before a beam of light began searching the backyard. She could hear Francis calling out for her, shouting her name, making promises she knew he wouldn't be able to keep. Laura took one last chance, reached through, and was able to stack the loose boards back over the hole. They wouldn't pass a close inspection, but right now, in the dark, it may be enough to conceal her route.

Straining her eyes, she searched the neighbor's backyard. Less than fifty feet wide, covered with tall grass, and an overgrown garden at the back, it had a similar layout. She squinted, spotting a dark shadowed area in the corner—a large garden shed. Laura clenched her jaw; it could work … it *had* to work. She ran across the yard, dragging Katy behind her, imagining a swarm of Reds already storming the house, finding their dead witch, and releasing the hounds into the yard to search for her. There would be no sparing her now, no second chances.

She tried to think of the brief survival lessons on evasion they taught her back at the base—what to do if they were attacked, if the Deltas got into the base and she had to escape. Back then she had a rifle and they taught her to use it, but even the military instructor training them knew the rifle would be her last resort. It was drilled into her that her best defense was to hide, and that's exactly what she would do now. She approached the garden shed and found the door locked with a pin. It was easily removed, but she would have no way to re-lock it from the inside. The door would open freely without it.

The door slid open like a barn; she dragged it just enough so that she could slip inside. She guided Katy in behind her and let the barn door slide shut. Moonlight shone in through a small skylight placed in the roof and a row of smaller windows in the front. She looked around the space, gasping and out of breath. Her eyes watered as she tried to focus on the room in front of her. Laura crept over the wooden floor of the small shed and past a rusted garden tractor parked in the center. In the back was an assortment of garden tools and burlap feed bags. Laura pressed in between the bags and sat Katy on the floor.

Laura flinched when she felt a static pulse through the knowledge cap. Her hand gripped it and she pulled and tugged, trying to remove it. The thing was solid, gripping her skull tightly. On the far wall, she saw a workbench, and near it was a large tool chest. Laura knelt close and pressed her face against

Katy's. "Stay here, hun. Momma has to do something."

Silently, Katy nodded her head. Laura forced a smile and kissed her forehead then crept across the space to the bench, feeling the static increase in her head. She knew it would have to be removed before they found her or crippled her with the cap. Finding a flat-tip screwdriver, she pried at the metallic device until her scalp bled, but the cap refused to move. She began to panic as the pressure in her skull increased. She searched the walls and saw a string of jumper cables hanging from a hook.

Taking the cables, she moved back to the garden tractor in the center of the room and lifted the tractor's seat, finding a small 12-volt battery right where she hoped it would be. She began breathing heavily, feeling the rush of pressure from the cap as it blocked the fear of what she was about to do. She connected the ends to the tractor battery then placed the negative on her cap. She looked in the corner where she'd left Katy, smiled, and then touched the positive clip to her cap.

There was no explosion or arc of electrical sparks like she expected; just the pain of a sledge hammer coming down on the base of her neck. She fell backwards and tumbled to the wooden floor. Instinctively, she reached up to touch her sore head and noticed the plate was gone. She found it on the floor beside her, the surface of the gold plate scorched where the electrical connection was made.

She lay on the floor, her cheek pressed against the dry boards. Katy ran to her side and palmed her face. "Are you okay, Momma?" she whispered.

Laura reached up and held the girl's hand. "I'm fine now."

There was a noise from outside, a splintering of wood that she knew was the clapboard fence. From her angle, she could just see under the sliding door and watched as heavy boots stomped through the yard in her direction. A bright light passed over the door, breaking through gaps in the shed's siding. She sat up and pulled Katy onto her lap, letting her eyes search the small space for a place to hide. Panicking, she knew it was hopeless; they were sure to find her.

Backing away, she scooched into the feedbags, pulling them in front of her. She heard hands grab the door, the wood clacking as something attempted to open it. The door slid partway before a distant explosion paused its motion. Laura heard human screams and gunshots followed by a man's voice shouting challenges. Holes appeared in the door where bullets pierced the wood, and a blue flash filled the gaps with light.

More gunfire and explosions covered the sounds of human screams. Laura crept toward the door and peeked out. An alien soldier in a blue uniform with red sleeves lay dead. Another was sitting against the clapboard fence a distance away, its hands grasping its bleeding chest. Laura slid the door open and looked out, seeing bright flashes of explosions over the rooftops of the homes. In the space between the houses, a man was kneeling as he held a pistol and was firing into the street.

She watched as blue bolts raced around him. The man stood his ground, covering groups of fleeing civilians who had previously lined up to enter the transports. Laura called to Katy and lifted the girl to her chest. Now was her chance; she would mix in with the fleeing group and leave with them. She ran through the yard, racing along the side of the house. As she drew near, she saw more uniformed men with rifles squaring off against the aliens. She turned and ran into the street. Just before she reached the man with the pistol, she watched as he was hit in the chest by a blue bolt, his torso melting under the flame of it.

The man fell back, his body hitting the ground. Laura watched his pistol slide across the pavement. She rushed toward the body, quickly scooped up the weapon, and tucked into the waist of her pants as she ran past him. Holding Katy tight, she found her way into the mass of fleeing civilians and tried to disappear into the group. It was chaotic, all of them running for a distant gate at the end of the street. Seeing the soldiers, their soldiers, fighting back against the aliens, she thought of Jacob. Laura tried to search the human faces for her husband, hoping he was alive and safe.

Running closer to the gate, she saw the uniformed men exchanging fire with the red-sleeved soldiers, the men desperately trying to create an exit for the civilians to escape through. The Deltas were clustering and stampeding into the opening, trying to plug the gap. A small car raced through the gate from outside, charging directly at the horde of Deltas. Bodies broke and were tossed aside as the car hit them, knocking several back and creating a wake of death in its path. The car reached the center of the horde and screeched to a stop. The Deltas swarmed and piled onto it before the car exploded into a blinding fireball. The blast knocked Laura back, the blinding flash pushing a shockwave over the crowd.

The crowd of civilians broke up and scattered, panicked men and women breaking in all directions. She followed a group of women behind a house. Holding Katy to her chest, she struggled to keep up with them. Laura didn't know where they were going, but she didn't want to be alone and she wanted to get away from the frantic fighting at the gate. She was rocked by a round of deafening explosions and felt the ground shudder.

"The wall is down!" a man ahead of her screamed, pointing to the far off structure. As he'd said, Laura could see that a large hole had been punched into it. Engulfed in bright yellow flames, the skeleton of a large fuel truck rolled through the breach.

The crowd turned and headed for the breach, desperate for a way out. Laura felt a hand grab her as a man's voice called her name; she turned and stared into the face of Francis. She reeled back, keeping Katy away from him. He held his hand out to her and said, "Come with me, there is still time to escape."

Laura backed up, not speaking and shaking her head.

"It's okay. I understand why you did what you did," he said, looking at her with compassion. "Please, this is all getting out of control. I have a transport; we can escape together."

An attack helicopter flew in close overhead, flying low over the group. The civilians ducked and cheered as the small aircraft made a gun run against the orb in the center of the community. As Laura stood and looked toward it, she let a smile cross her face.

"Are you enjoying this?" Francis shouted at her.

Laura stepped back and turned toward the breach, trying to catch up with the group. Francis again reached out and grabbed her arm, this time pulling her back violently. "You're coming with me!" he said sternly.

Katy gripped her neck tightly and began to scream. Laura was spun back so quickly she lost her footing and was tugged into the man. He looked her in the eye, putting his face close to hers. "I'm not giving you the choice; you're coming with me."

Laura let her right arm drift to her waist while still struggling to pull away from Francis. She found the pistol and grasped it tightly. She tugged and broke his grip. He lashed out and smacked her face with the back of his hand. She felt the sting and tasted the blood on her lip. She paused and glared at him. He held a stone expression. "Come. There isn't time."

Laura shook her head and raised her right hand. Francis saw the pistol, his eyes going wide. "I always knew my end would come this way," he said.

She squeezed the trigger, hitting him in the chest. His hands reached up at his light-blue robe, the blood seeping between his fingers. He dropped to his knees and eyed up at her. He shook his head and stared down at the grass. People ran past them, rushing for the breach in the wall. Laura backed away as he reached out his blood-covered hand. "It didn't have to be this way."

It was just then that Francis lunged for her. Laura stumbled back and again pulled the trigger. She watched as Francis's head snapped back with a hole in the center of his face. She suddenly felt weak in her legs, and Katy felt very heavy against her chest.

A large woman stopped beside her. "Come on, keep going; we're almost out."

Laura looked into the woman's hard eyes. The lady was dressed in civilian clothing; dirt and blood coated her forehead. She was husky and had the look of a leader, her black and gray hair tied back, scarf hanging loosely from her neck. The older woman traveled with several other young girls as a group, like a family. Laura nodded and turned to follow her.

As they got closer to the gate, men rushed through to greet them from several open-backed trucks that sat parked in the breach. Helicopters raced overhead, dodging the bolts of blue plasma as they provided supporting fire to the men on the ground. Ahead, a man was standing in the high grass, directing the loading of vehicles as another man rallied soldiers to press on toward the battle near the orb. Laura stayed close to the woman, letting her lead the way to safety.

"Clem," the husky woman shouted to one of the soldiers. Laura stopped and stood close with the others. The man glanced back then reached out and hugged the woman. "Ruth! I thought you got it back at the warehouse."

The woman shook her head. "I should have. I was knocked out when our truck rolled, and I woke up here."

Laura pushed past them and grabbed the man's oilskin coat. "I remember you," she said. "You were at the cabin; you left with my husband. Do you know where he is?"

Clem pursed his lips, looking at her and the young girl on her chest. He nodded and pointed at the far off gate where the battle still raged. "He's in there, leading the fight."

Laura turned and looked back, seeing the waves of Deltas and Reds rushing at the men dug in on the line, fighting against them as waves of helicopters roared overhead.

Clem put a hand on her shoulder. "Come on, we need to get you all out of here."

Chapter 29

The transport moved forward on a cushion of air, rocked back with the shockwaves of nearby explosions. Rogers was sitting by Karina's side, directing her path through the maze of rallied soldiers. The nearby men—some hiding in the woods; others, survivors and remnants from Meaford—had answered the call. Every unit and militiaman within fifty miles had come out of hiding to join the fight, all of them coming together in one last stand against the alien base.

James was standing in the open hatch, wearing one of the red-sleeved uniform jackets over his own uniform, running a heavy machine gun. He dropped back into the hatch just as a splash of blue harmlessly bounced off the surface of the hovercraft.

"You sure we're safe in here, and wearing this shit, Karina?" James shouted, hesitating before he climbed back out of the hatch.

The guide was busy driving the vehicle and didn't answer. Looking through the large, viewscreen display, Jacob could see the chaos outside. All types of civilian and military vehicles were rushing by them on all sides. Columns of advancing troops were firing into the open gate as they moved forward. He even saw helicopters from some hidden base had joined the last-ditch fight against the invaders.

"This vehicle, and the Ursus' uniforms, have thermal shielding; highly effective against the Ursus' rifles," Karina finally said. A burst of rounds pinged and crunched against the side of the transport, followed by a blast of sparks and smoke popping from a console on the bulkhead. "Unfortunately, we were not prepared for your high-velocity projectile weapons."

"Well, that was stupid," James laughed.

Jacob was also wearing one of the Ursus' jackets. It had the feel of smooth synthetic leather; it was light and seemed to shrink and adjust to the occupant's size. They'd used shoe polish to cover the red-striped sleeves in hopes that an excited soldier wouldn't put a bullet into them. The pock-marked and blood-stained front of Jacob's jacket reminded him that these coats wouldn't work against a good old fashioned rifle. They'd procured the enemy armor, but the rifles were useless to them. Somehow tuned in to the alien DNA, their own human bodies were unable to activate them.

She shook her head, thrusting the vehicle forward, narrowly missing a car racing into a Delta horde at high speed. "The last time we visited this world, the most advance projectile we faced was a musket or a spear." The craft rocked as it collided with a truck; she corrected course and directed it forward. "We would have expected your weapons to evolve with your technology—lasers or other energy-based weapons—but you humans have embraced your primitive projectiles."

James laughed loudly, loading another belt of ammo into his M240. "Hell, yeah!" he shouted. "We love guns." He stood and climbed back into the turret, firing long salvos into the Delta horde.

Jacob watched on the view screen as a column of small cars raced directly into the Deltas and exploded in the center of the mass. Karina ducked as the view screen filled with the devastation, the explosion temporarily washing out the display. Rogers righted her, putting her back on the controls. "Militias," Rogers said, pointing to the craters left by the car bombs. "They are not to be fucked with."

She put her head down, working the throttle and veering to the left to allow more of the car bombers to pass by her. "I will never understand your people's call to violence. Why not just leave? Even if you win here, you cannot win everywhere."

Rogers grunted. "Look who's talking. Those men out there fighting have had everything taken away from them. *Your* people created this, not ours. You said it yourself; if we leave, they'll cull this area with The Darkness. Maybe we can stop that."

"You are only delaying the inevitable. The exodus has begun; there is no way for you to win once our main forces arrive. This is a waste of both of our people," Karina protested as she watched the slaughter in front of her.

Rogers looked up and saw they were now at the stalled front lines. Ahead of them, men were exchanging gunfire with the aliens at long range. In the distance, he could just make out the glow of the alien orb. "Okay, this is close enough. We can move out on foot from here."

With that, Karina broke the craft from its hover. Slamming a control arm forward, the vehicle anchored hard into the ground outside and came to rest, grinding against the earth below them. James's machine gun continued to rattle away, spilling hot brass into the compartment. Duke paced and growled below, snapping at the man's boots while Karina used a control panel to drop the rear ramp. Jacob lifted his rifle close to his chest and checked the action. He turned and followed Rogers out as the big man moved Karina ahead of him into the open battlefield. The sounds of war were louder outside, the air filled with the zipping of rounds, yelling of men, and the stench of burning explosives and gunpowder.

Overhead a Blackhawk passed by at high speed, gunners firing from the doors. The bird banked hard, making a dangerously close pass while the door gunners bled rounds into the last of the Delta lines. In front of the horde, the remnants of one of Meaford's remaining rifle battalions were in close, engaging The Darkness at point-blank range.

"They teach you about close air support at your Star Fleet Academy?" Rogers said, smiling at the helicopters racing overhead. "I notice you turds don't have any air defense."

She shook her head. "Like I said … spears and muskets. But you can trust me when I tell you that our main forces will have such things. These skies will not be safe when the exodus arrives."

Rogers moved around the side of the hovercraft; he squatted and waited for the others to catch up then peeked around the corner. Just as Karina had said, the defenders appeared to be pulling back. Off to the right was a series of loud explosions that rocked the ground and lit the sky to the east in balls of orange flame. He turned his gaze and pointed to a section of the alien wall, now crumbled and twisted. "That would be Clem. Right on time, opening another exit."

Jacob stood and used the optics of his rifle to look in the direction of the blast, seeing the bright fireballs of exploding semi-trucks laden with explosives. The wall was peeled back in an open breach. Transport trucks raced through to gather the fleeing civilians. He searched the mass and could see long columns of approaching survivors. Jacob held his breath and prayed that Katy and Laura were in the group.

"You okay, Jake?" Rogers called back to him.

Jacob lowered his rifle; he closed his eyes, feeling his muscles tighten. He swallowed hard, knowing that they were exacting a hard revenge for everything that had been done to them. "On it, boss. Let's get this done," he said, pulling his rifle into his shoulder.

Rogers slapped James on the shoulder, the man now having switched out the heavy machine gun for a carbine, Duke by his side and ready to move. "Lead us out, James," Rogers said.

James grimaced and stepped off, running ahead at a jog with Duke beside him. Rogers led Karina ahead of him as they fell in with pockets of other soldiers advancing forward. The team ducked down a narrow street and headed for the main road that would take them in the direction of the orb. Jacob followed with his rifle up, covering the way. The

Delta resistance had been broken; any of the remaining black-eyed creatures were now separated into small pockets and easily cut down by the approaching soldiers.

The Ursus were nowhere to be seen. The way ahead apeared clear, with an empty street all the way to the orb. “Where the hell are your friends?” Rogers barked after they’d reached a narrow street flanked by small cookie-cutter homes.

Karina stopped and looked ahead pointing. “They will set their final defense in the landing ship.” She turned back to Rogers. “Please … you must give them the opportunity to submit.”

Rogers shot her a hateful glare. “Like the one you gave us at Meaford?” He turned and signaled for James to press ahead into the quiet neighborhoods.

Along the route, the men stopped to pound on doors while others provided security. Along the outer walls, they could still hear heavy fighting as The Darkness drew toward the fighting in the community. Soldiers were working desperately to evacuate the last remaining civilians from the community, showing them the way out.

Jacob passed by the fleeing civilians, checking every face as the people passed by. He was still surprised at the way the base fell and the inability of the invaders to put up a solid defense. “Karina, where is everyone? You must have more than this," Jacob asked her as she trudged along beside him with her head down.

"Only two legions came down with the lander; we rely heavily on the witnesses for defense," she said. "Your people have killed many of the Ursus in the field."

"Why haven't they sent reinforcements?" Rogers asked.

She stopped and rubbed her eyes, taking in a deep breath. "When our Messenger was killed at the reception ceremony, it brought great shame on this communal. Not only that, but it brought great attention on our failures. The council decided to write this place off, determining the population too dangerous for habitation. There will be no reinforcements."

"You know, I was the one that tagged that fruit cake," James grunted, overhearing the conversation.

She looked at him, puzzled.

"Your Messiah character, that was me," James boasted proudly. "Easy shooting too. Right through the brain bucket. Split the dude's grape wide open then punched two more into his chest for good measure."

Karina turned away, horrified. "When you killed the Messenger, you took away the communal's means of negotiation; only the Messenger has the privilege to settle for peace with the local population."

James laughed and spit on the ground near her feet. "Some luck, huh?" He grunted and moved away, not expecting a response.

Uniformed men were bounding forward, moving tactically toward the final perimeter near the outer edges of the orb. James guided them through what appeared to be an alien motor pool divided into cubes. The nearby soldiers were swiftly moving the last pocket of survivors to safety through the maze of heavy rock barriers that separated sections of the motor pool from other areas while Jacob's team moved into an empty bay that overlooked the front entrance to the orb.

No longer glowing, Rogers noted the dull object's hatches and exits were sealed. A small balcony that ran along the roof of the object revealed small groups of the Ursus soldiers. They appeared to be randomly engaging the men on the ground with pot shots. Rogers quickly fell back into cover beside the others. An organized unit of combat engineers was moving ahead, supported by a Stryker vehicle, its 30mm gun blasting away at the sides of the ship.

Suddenly, the main hatch of the orb fell back. The void quickly filled with a large vehicle equipped with a massive turret that opened up with its main gun, destroying the Stryker with waves of plasma. The vehicle drew fire as it raced down the ramp to engage the engineers on the ground. The red-sleeved soldiers used the frenzied action to try to gain momentum. They poured out of the orb, firing at the dug in soldiers surrounding them.

"You must stop this," Karina pleaded with Rogers. "Pull back! This fight is already over."

Rogers shook his head. "No, we have to end this place and keep them from creating more of the Deltas."

Karina's eyes couldn't grow any wider. She grabbed at Rogers, pleading with him to stop the killing. Ignoring her, he turned away. A group of soldiers ran to their position and knelt down next to Rogers. A sergeant leaned in close to report. "We have all of the survivors located. These are the last of the enemy holdouts; we finish them off and were clear to egress. The captain wants to know if there is anything your scouts can do to assist us in assaulting the craft."

Without warning, the enemy fire intensified. Another hatch opened and a second assault vehicle rushed out of the orb, leading a wave of Ursus into the open. A soldier escorting the reporting sergeant was hit with splatter from the blue plasma; his face vanished in a hot flash. Rogers drew the other soldier deeper into cover before rising up to return fire.

Jacob watched in horror as a group of civilians were caught in the open. A man sprinted to the barrier, carrying a child in his arms. A Red directed several pulses at the man, narrowly missing yet causing the man to trip and roll to his back. The Ursus concentrated their fire in the man's direction as he scrambled to get his child into cover. Jacob jumped over the barrier he was hiding behind, James yelling for him to get back. Under intense fire with the blue bolts raining down on them from elevated positions, Jacob made it to the forward cover. He rose up, firing rapidly to suppress the aliens on the catwalk while screaming for the man and child to move.

Watching them get to cover, he tried to escape himself by crawling to a corner of the low wall then rising up again to fire back; this time his luck ran out and he was hit in the flank by a blast of plasma. He tumbled back, the air knocked from his lungs as he rolled behind the stone barrier. The Ursus's armored jacket held, but he felt the blazing heat against his skin under his left arm.

The fire to his front stopped with the Ursus assuming he was dead, angering Jacob even more than being shot at. He clenched his teeth and checked the action on his rifle then rolled out of cover. He spotted the Red, now focused on his team. Jacob centered the cross hair and squeezed the trigger, proudly observing as the side of the alien's helmet exploded outward.

The aliens appeared to be making a last push to retake the communal. "We have to get these people out of here," the soldier yelled, pointing to a pinned down group of civilians behind them. He rolled to his left and back into cover, looking to the wall behind him and the huddled group of women and children. They reminded him of his family, and he immediately wondered if they'd gotten out safe.

Rogers turned to him and pointed to a parked alien transport in another of the sheltered bays farther away from the outer walls of the orb. "Jacob, take it and get these people to the coast."

Jacob shook his head. "No. I'm staying, dammit. Have somebody else do it. Besides, I can't drive one of those things."

Rogers shook his head. "It wasn't a suggestion; I'm telling you. Now take Karina and go. Get those people to safety. Meet up with Clem at the coast. If you hurry, you'll get there before he leaves."

Jacob hesitated and Rogers grabbed him by the shoulders, pulling him in. "Go. I'll catch up with you later," he said. "Don't worry about us. Once we finish here, we'll be right behind you."

Jacob nodded and raised his fist to meet Rogers's. "See ya soon then," he said, and ran off with Karina toward the hovercraft.

Chapter 30

The transport crunched over debris as it moved toward the coastline. Jacob sat on top, surrounded by survivors who sat or stood anywhere they could find a spot atop the hovercraft. The vehicle was loaded to capacity. The compartment below was filled and they had kept the ramp open and dragged it behind them to allow more to ride along. The road was quiet; they hadn't seen any of the enemy since leaving the walls of the communal. As the sun rose on the horizon, Jacob wondered what would come. Would the enemy send more to recapture it, or just let the place be?

Ahead, they spotted columns of civilians marching along the side of the road. They scattered upon feeling the ear tickles of the hovercraft, but then turned back, looking curiously to watch the alien vehicle covered with humans. Word had spread to get to the marinas on the coast if any survivors in the area wanted to leave.

Soon, the road was filled with walking crowds of people carrying all of their belongings. Once the road became too choked with people to proceed, Karina moved the hovercraft to the shoulder and they abandoned the vehicle. Jacob led her away, walking into the wood line, and kept her out of sight while he searched through discarded luggage and bags on the side of the road.

Jacob returned to her with a handful of clothing and children's jackets recovered from the road. She was very small for a human woman, but Jacob figured she could easily pass for a young adult in the right light. He handed her a small, brightly colored jacket with a large hood he'd picked and stood watch while she changed into the new clothing.

As she made to rejoin him on the road, Jacob stopped and turned to face her. "I won't make you stay with me. You are free to go."

Karina frowned at him. "My people would refuse me now. I have nowhere to go, but I could help you."

"How?"

"I can remove the knowledge plates—the caps. There are other things I could do. Don't abandon me here."

Jacob shrugged, having no sympathy for her. He turned away and continued walking toward the coast. Looking back, he saw that she was following just behind him. “Will they come back?” he asked her.

Karina moved up, keeping pace with him. “They will be forced to respond. The musing transports systems showed areas south of here that are secure and safe, but the North has been declared too cold for our people. I suggest we go there.”

Jacob didn’t answer her; this wasn’t new information. Although he suspected the real reason they wouldn’t move north was because the Deltas didn’t do well in the cold water. He smiled, wondering if they knew what Chicago and Michigan would be like when winter came. Maybe the ice on the lakes would freeze them all out. He lost himself in thought while walking with the group. When he looked around, he realized he’d picked up a following—people recognized his uniform and were falling in around him. Walking with him, were people desperate for any sort of structure in the chaos.

Ahead, the woods began to thin, destroyed vehicles lined the road, and the packs of people grew into uncountable numbers. He could see the waterline and the makings of a harbor. Survivors were lined up and being escorted into boats then ferried out to large vessels anchored in the bay. He had a flash of déjà vu, remembering a similar flotilla in Lake Michigan of the waters of Chicago. He stopped and stared at the impressive sight, allowing the others to move past him to meander down the road and fall into the lines.

He saw more armed men, militia and soldiers standing watch over the lines and guiding the survivors to the boats. Karina stood beside him. “It could have been different,” she said.

“Your people made that choice, not mine.”

She nodded and moved ahead. Jacob rolled his shoulders and followed her. He found the back of the lines and moved past them, continuing on to a group of soldiers near the head of a pier. Men with clipboards were taking a head count of families before leading them down the pier to waiting passenger ferries. Jacob recognized the unit patch from Meaford and stepped close to the soldier.

“I’m looking for a woman and her daughter.”

The soldier looked up at him with a cross expression; he waved the clipboard at the long line of people. “Take your pick.”

Jacob nodded his head and exhaled, beginning to turn away.

“Hold up,” the man said, putting a hand on Jacob’s shoulder. He pointed to a small ticket office at the head of the pier. “Check in at the office. We turn these registers into Laura; she's been keeping track of everyone board—"

"Wait," Jacob interrupted, his face breaking into a smile. He grabbed the man by both shoulders. "Laura, is that what you said her name was?"

The man nodded. "Yeah …" He looked at Jacob as recollection filled his eyes. "As a matter of fact, she has a little girl too. Nahh, man, you gotta be shitting me. That's who you're looking for?"

Jacob spun away. Dropping his pack, he ran for the ticket office placed just to the right of the pier walkway. Jacob moved around piles of luggage and empty boxes. The building was square and painted white; the front held a glass ticket counter, the glass now covered with heavy cardboard. Jacob skirted around the building and found a small door where a soldier stood outside it, smoking a cigarette. He saw Jacob approach and eyed up at him.

"Something I can—Anderson?!" Masterson said, looking at him with shock. "How in the hell …? Are the others with you?"

Jacob shook his head. "Is she in there?" Jacob asked.

Masterson flipped his cigarette into the water and turned back. He reached behind him, opened the door, and allowed Jacob to move ahead of him.

Inside, the room was low lit and dusty. A tired sergeant sat behind a desk, going over charts and stacks of papers, and a second man lay sleeping on a bench with his rifle and rucksack beside him.

"Through that door," Masterson said, pointing to a door set into the back of the room, *Manager* stenciled on the old wood.

Speechless now, he felt the anticipation building in his guts. He stepped to the door and grabbed the knob. Pausing, he took a deep breath and pushed the door in, following it into the room. She was there, going over stacks of papers and transposing names into a large journal book. She heard the door but didn't look up. "You can set the papers over there," she said, pointing to a large box filled with the unbound pages.

When Jacob didn't reply, she looked up and her jaw dropped.

"How …? When …?" she gasped. Pushing away from the desk, she ran to him.

Jacob wrapped his arms around her, pulling her in tight. "I just got here. The men out front told me the way."

She stood wrapped in his embrace. "I love you," she said, looking up into his stubbled and scarred face. Pressing her close to him, he kissed her, and for the moment they were safe and far away.

"How did you get here?"

"Kiss me again," she said.

He met her lips, closing his eyes and letting the warmth of the room take him. He felt a tug and heard a call from Katy. He dropped to her level and lifted her in a tight hug. "Daddy! You're back," she said, tears in her eyes.

"I'm back, Katy," he said, the three of them now wrapped up together.

Epilogue

On a cold pre-dawn morning, water slapped against the sides of a tall, double-decked cabin cruiser. The boat rested low in the water at the outer edge of the floating refugee camp. Every day, the floating city grew smaller as vessels of every type broke off and plotted a course to move northwest toward Michigan's Upper Peninsula—the last known safe area for humans.

For reasons unknown, the aliens had stopped moving to the northern parts of the state. Rumors thought it had to do with the dioxin attacks in central Michigan. Others claimed that the creatures were unable to adapt to the cold climates. Some even claimed the creatures had learned a lesson with the losses there, and Jacob suspected the trend had occurred in other areas as well.

Jacob stood at the controls, watching a large fishing trawler pull away, black smoke rising from its stack as white water churned up in the wake of the departing ship. Another group in search of a safe place to start over. He watched as the vessel faded away, hoping they would find the safety they were searching for.

Counting the dwindling number of vessels remaining, he contemplated how long he would be able to wait for them. But after everything they'd done, they deserved his patience. He sat down and looked up at the sky, forgetting how many stars were up there. He would never look at them the same way again. A tracer cut across the horizon, another easily identified as a Karinan vessel. They'd named the alien race—with much objection from her—after their traveling companion. Karina was correct in her predictions of the exodus. Ships were entering orbit daily, flying overhead and buzzing the flotilla. So far they had left them alone. Karina said they wouldn't attack unless their territories were entered, for now anyway. She claimed that most of the people fleeing the dying galaxy would have no stomach for the fighting. Jacob had his doubts, but maybe she was telling the truth.

The sun broke the horizon to his back and lit a shining path across the water. He focused on a far off vessel; rather than departing, this one was coming closer. He heard Laura below deck moving through the cabin; she stepped lightly on the steps and stood beside him then handed him a cup of instant coffee. He could hear Karina and Katy laughing below in the galley while fixing the morning meal. Jacob pointed out the approaching vessel to Laura. She moved closer and put her arm around his waist, watching silently.

He slowly began to recognize the ship and remember where he'd seen it last. On a mission to the east coast of Michigan. A Navy vessel that transported them across these same dangerous waters. He stepped off the bridge, grabbed a small pair of binoculars, and climbed up to the second deck. He steadied his eye and focused on the bow. His body warmed when he saw men on the bow leaning against the rail, the shape of a dog standing with them. He smiled and turned to the controls, starting the engine.

"What are you doing?" Laura called from below.

He looked down at her excitedly. "They're back."

***

The height of winter, they strolled the shoreline of Mackinaw Island. In the distance, an ice bridge had formed and teams were moving supplies across the Straits of Mackinaw from the mainland aboard horse-drawn sleds. Standing alone and closer to the tree line, Jacob watched them. He found a worn driftwood log and sat atop it, letting his rifle hang loose from the sling. He grinned while watching Katy roll through the snow as the big bearded man and scout dog dropped to make snow angels on the beach with her.

The remaining members of the Assassins had claimed one of the large homes overlooking the lake. Soon after, other survivors arrived, retaking the town and bringing the area back to life. They hoped to again have steady electrical power, but for now they relied on the generators. James still left quite often with his Delta detecting dog, making trips to the southern part of the state to check on his friends at the bunker where a large Army outpost had now been established—the threat of the dioxin still keeping the aliens away.

The radio traffic called the survivors *holdouts* and *the last bastions of humanity*. James's favorite word for them was *insurgents*. Invitations were often sent to them by courier, asking them to return home. Celebrities and political figures made recordings that were broadcast over the radio, asking for the *holdouts* and those like them to lay down their weapons and return to the south to live in the well-structured communities of the Karinans. Instead of becoming a deterrent, they motivated others to flee the communal and make the trek north to the safety of the human camps. Knowing that others were surviving on their own motivated families to take the risk and flee.

The word the humans gave to the alien people had become a slur to them. Named for what the humans considered a hero of their race and what the aliens considered a traitor, Karina was now an ambassador to the free peoples of North America. She was protected and kept safe, yet always on the move. Rogers traveled with her from camp to camp, keeping up the morale and building support for the resistance. They'd manage to salvage bits of alien technology and even recovered a fully functioning orb in North Dakota. With Karina's help, they also managed a way to convert the Ursus battle rifles for human use.

Katy stood and waved to him, laughing before she turned back to tackle Duke, the two of them tumbling into the heavy snow. He heard the crunching of boots and looked behind him. Laura appeared, carrying a long thermos. She grinned and poured him a cup of hot chocolate then dropped to sit beside him on the log. They had as much of everything as they needed. With the threat of The Darkness retreating in the wake of the winter snow, they'd been able to raid food warehouses all along the state. Supermarkets and corner stores still sat full with their stores of canned goods. There would be plenty of food for the winters, and they'd have time to grow their own in the coming spring.

James ran toward them, carrying Katy in his arms and Duke bounding by his side. His beard and jacket covered in snow, he looked like the abominable snowman. He pointed to the cup in Jacob's hand and scowled. "Hey, Mom and Dad, you're holding out on us!"

Laura laughed before pouring them each a cup then turned to Jacob and hugged him close. "I think we're going to be okay here," she said.

The End

I hope you enjoyed ***The Shadows,*** and would consider leaving a **review**.

W. J. Lundy is a still serving Veteran of the U.S. Military with service in Afghanistan. He has over 15 years of combined service with the Army and Navy in Europe, the Balkans and Southwest Asia. Visit him on **Facebook** for more.

Other works by:

WJ Lundy

WHISKEY TANGO FOXTROT SERIES

Escaping the Dead

Tales of the Forgotten

Only the Dead Live Forever

Walking in the Shadow of Death

Something to Fight For

Divided We Fall

OTHER AUTHORS UNDER THE SHIELD OF

SIXTH CYCLE

Nuclear war has destroyed human civilization.
Captain Jake Phillips wakes into a dangerous new world, where he finds the remaining fragments of the population living in a series of strongholds, connected across the country. Uneasy alliances have maintained their safety, but things are about to change. -- Discovery **leads to danger.** -- Skye Reed, a tracker from the Omega stronghold, uncovers a threat that could spell the end for their fragile society. With friends and enemies revealing truths about the past, she will need to decide who to trust. -- Sixth **Cycle** is a gritty post-apocalyptic story of survival and adventure.

Darren Wearmouth ~ Carl Sinclair

DEAD ISLAND: Operation Zulu

Ten years after the world was nearly brought to its knees by a zombie Armageddon, there is a race for the antidote! On a remote Caribbean island, surrounded by a horde of hungry living dead, a team of American and Australian commandos must rescue the Antidotes' scientist. Filled with zombies, guns, Russian bad guys, shady government types, serial killers and elevator muzak. Dead Island is an action packed blood soaked horror adventure.

Allen Gamboa

INVASION OF THE DEAD SERIES

This is the first book in a series of nine, about an ordinary bunch of friends, and their plight to survive an apocalypse in Australia. -- Deep beneath defense headquarters in the Australian Capital Territory, the last ranking Army chief and a brilliant scientist struggle with answers to the collapse of the world, and the aftermath of an unprecedented virus. Is it a natural mutation, or does the infection contain -- more sinister roots? -- One hundred and fifty miles away, five friends returning from a month-long camping trip slowly discover that death has swept through the country. What greets them in a gradual revelation is an enemy beyond compare. -- Armed with dwindling ammunition, the friends must overcome their disagreements, utilize their individual skills, and face unimaginable horrors as they battle to reach their hometown...

Owen Ballie

Whiskey Tango Foxtrot

Alone in a foreign land. The radio goes quiet while on convoy in Afghanistan, a lost patrol alone in the desert. With his unit and his home base destroyed, Staff Sergeant Brad Thompson suddenly finds himself isolated and in command of a small group of men trying to survive in the Afghan wasteland. **Every turn leads to danger**

The local population has been afflicted with an illness that turns them into rabid animals. They pursue him and his men at every corner and stop. Struggling to hold his team together and unite survivors, he must fight and evade his way to safety. **A fast paced zombie war story like no other.**

W.J. Lundy

ZOMBIE RUSH

New to the Hot Springs PD Lisa Reynolds was not all that welcomed by her coworkers especially those who were passed over for the position. It didn't matter, her thirty days probation ended on the same day of the Z-poc's arrival. Overnight the world goes from bad to worse as thousands die in the initial onslaught. National Guard and regular military unit deployed the day before to the north leaves the city in mayhem. All directions lead to death until one unlikely candidate steps forward with a plan. A plan that became an avalanche raging down the mountain culminating in the salvation or destruction of them all.

Joseph Hansen

THE ALPHA PLAGUE

Rhys is an average guy who works an average job in Summit City—a purpose built government complex on the outskirts of London. The Alpha Tower stands in the centre of the city. An enigma, nobody knows what happens behind its dark glass. Rhys is about to find out. At ground zero and with chaos spilling out into the street, Rhys has the slightest of head starts. If he can remain ahead of the pandemonium, then maybe he can get to his loved ones before the plague does. The Alpha Plague is a post-apocalyptic survival thriller.

Michael Robertson

THE GATHERING HORDE

The most ambitious terrorist plot ever undertaken is about to be put into motion, releasing an unstoppable force against humanity. Ordinary people – A group of students celebrating the end of the semester, suburban and rural families – are about to themselves in the center of something that threatens the survival of the human species. As they battle the dead – and the living – it's going to take every bit of skill, knowledge and luck for them to survive in Zed's World.

Rich Baker

THE FORGOTTEN LAND

Sergeant Steve Golburn, an Australian Special Air Service veteran, is tasked with a dangerous mission in Iraq, deep behind enemy lines. When Steve's five man SAS patrol inadvertently spark a time portal, they find themselves in 10th century Viking Denmark. A place far more dangerous and lawless than modern Iraq. Join the SAS patrol on this action adventure into the depths of not only a hostile land, far away from the support of the Allied front line, but into another world…another time.

Keith McArdle

Made in the USA
Las Vegas, NV
15 April 2021

21468797R00177